THE THING FROM THE LAKE

THE THING FROM THE LAKE

ELEANOR MARIE INGRAM

ISBN: 978-93-5342-925-6

First Published: -

LECTOR HOUSE LLP
E-MAIL: lectorpublishing@gmail.com

THE THING FROM THE LAKE

BY

ELEANOR M. INGRAM

Author of "From the Car Behind", "The Unafraid", etc.

CONTENTS

CONTENTS

CHAPTER I

"As well give up the Bible at once, as our belief in apparitions."

—Wesley.

The house cried out to me for help.

In the after-knowledge I now possess of what was to happen there, that impression is not more clearly definite than it was at my first sight of the place. Let me at once set down that this is not the story of a haunted house. It is, or was, a beleaguered house; strangely besieged as was Prague in the old legend, when a midnight army of spectres unfurled pale banners and encamped around the city walls.

Of course, I did not know all this, the day that my real-estate agent brought his little car to a stop before the dilapidated farm. I believed the house only appealed to be lived in; for deliverance from the destroying work of neglect and time. A spring rain was whispering down from a gray sky, dripping from broken gutters and eaves with a patter like timid footsteps hurrying by, yet even in the storm the house did not look dreary.

"There, Mr. Locke, is a bargain," the agent called back to me, where I sat in my car. "Finest bit in Connecticut for a city man's summer home! Woodland, farm land, lake and a house that only needs a few repairs to be up-to-date. Look at that double row of maples, sir. Shade all summer! Fine old orchard, too; with a trifle of attention."

I nodded, surveying the house with an eagerness of interest that surprised myself. A box-like, fairly large structure of commonplace New England ugliness, it coaxed my liking as had no other place I had ever seen; it wooed me like a determined woman. And as one would long to clothe beautifully a beloved woman, I looked at the house and foresaw what an architect could do for it; how creamy stucco; broad white porches and a gay scarlet roof would transform it.

"Come inside," my agent urged, hope in his voice as he observed my face; "let me show you the interior. I brought the keys along. Of course, the rooms may seem a bit musty. No one has lived in it for—some time. It's the old Michell property; been in the family for a couple of hundred years. Last Michell is dead, now, and it's being sold for the benefit of some religious institute the old gentleman left it to. Trifle wet to walk over the land today! But I've a plan and measurements in my portfolio."

I said that we would go in. If he had but known the fact, the place was already sold to me; before I left my car, before I entered the house, before I had seen the hundred-odd acres that make up the estate.

There was a narrow, flagged path to the veranda, where the planking moved and creaked under our weight while my companion unlocked the front door. Rather astonishingly, the air of the long-closed place was neither musty nor damp, when we stepped in. Instead, there was a faint, resinous odor, very pleasant and clean; perhaps from the cedar of which the woodwork largely consisted.

The house was partially furnished. Not, of course, with much that I would care to retain, but a few good antiques stood out among their commonplace associates. A large bedroom on the north side, which I appointed as my own at first sight, held an old rosewood set including a four-posted, pineapple-carved bed. I threw open the shutters in this room and looked out.

I received the first jar to my satisfaction. On this side of the place, the grounds ran down a slight slope for perhaps half a block to the five-acre hollow of shallow water and lush growth which the agent called a lake. From it flowed a considerable creek, winding behind the house and away on its journey to the Sound. For that under-water marsh I felt a shock of violent dislike.

"You don't care for the lake?" my companion deprecated, at my elbow. "Fine trout in that stream, though! I'd like you to see it in the sunshine."

"I should care more for it if it was a lake, not a swamp," I answered.

"Oh, but that is only because the old dam is down," he exclaimed eagerly. "That lets all the water out, you see. Why, if the dam were put back, you'd have as pretty a lake for a canoe as there is in the State! Its natural depth is four or five feet all over, and about eight or ten where the stream flows through to the dam. Even yet, a few wild duck stop there spring and fall, and when I was a boy I've seen heron. Put back the dam, Mr. Locke, and I'll guarantee you'll never say swamp again!"

"We will try it," I said. "Now let us find a lawyer and see how quickly I can be put in possession."

We drove back to the little town from which we had that morning started out, and where my agent lived; my sleek car following his small one with somewhat the effect of a long-limbed panther striding behind an agitated mouse.

It appeared that the sale was simply consummated. I do not mean that all the formalities were completed in a day. But by nightfall I could feel myself the owner of the place.

Perhaps it was the giddiness of being a land-owner for the first time, or perhaps it was the abject wretchedness of the only hotel in town that inspired the whim which seized me during my solitary dinner. I had spent one night here, and did not welcome the prospect of a second. A return to New York was not practicable, because I had arranged to meet several contractors and an architect at the farm, next morning, to discuss the alterations I wanted made. Why not drive out to my new house this evening and sleep tonight in the rosewood-furnished bedroom?

The idea gained favor as I contemplated it. I could go over the house tonight and sketch more clearly what I wanted done, while I would be on the ground when my men arrived next morning. There was an allure of camping out about it, too.

In the end I went, of course.

It was dark when I stabled my roadster in the barn that was part of my new possessions; where the car seemed to glitter disdain of the hay-littered, ragged shelter. Equipped with a flashlight, suitcase and bundle, I followed a faint path that wound its way to the house through wet blackberry vines whose thorns had outlived the winter. My steps broke the blank silence that brooded over the place. At this season there was no insect life; nor any other stirring thing within hearing or sight. But just as I stepped upon the veranda, I heard a vague sound from the lake that lay a few hundred feet to the north. There was no wind, yet the water had seemed to move with a sound like the smacking of soft, glutinous lips. Or as if some soft body drew itself from a bed of clinging mud. I wondered idly if the tide could run this far back from Long Island Sound.

The house reiterated the impression of welcoming me. I shut and locked the old door behind me, and went up to the room I had chosen as my own. There I unshuttered and opened the windows, lighted one of the candles I had brought and set it on a little bookcase filled with dingy volumes, and threw my blankets on the bed. I had moved in!

My pleasant sense of proprietorship continued to grow. Before I thought of sleep, I had been through the house several times from cellar to attic and accumulated a list of things to be done. Back in my room, an hour passed in revising the list, by candle-light.

Near ten o'clock, I rolled myself in a dressing-gown and my blankets, spread an automobile robe over the four-posted bed, and fell asleep.

CHAPTER II

"Beware of her fair hair, for she excels
All women in the magic of her locks."

—SHELLEY (*Trans.*).

It trailed suavely through my fingers, slipping across my palm like a belt of silk. It glided with the noiseless haste of a thing in flight. Quite naturally, even in the dazed moment of awakening I closed my hand upon it. It was soft in my grasp, yet resilient; solid, yet supple. If I may speak irrationally, it felt as if it must be fragrant. It was a strange visitor to my experience, yet I recognized its identity unerringly as a blind man gaining sight might identify a flower or a bird. In brief, it was—it only could be an opulent braid of hair.

When I grasped it, it ceased to move.

In the dense darkness of my bedroom, I lay still and considered. I was alone, or rather, should have been alone in the old house I had bought the day before. The agent assured me that it had been unoccupied for years. Who, then, was my guest? A passer-by seeking refuge in a supposedly deserted house would hardly have moved about with such silent caution. A tramp of this genus would be a rarity indeed. I had nothing with me of value to attract a thief. The usual limited masculine jewelry—a watch, a pair of cuff-links, a modest pin—surely were not sufficiently tempting to snare so dainty a bird of prey as one wearing such plumage as I held. I have not a small fist, yet that braid was a generous handful. How did it come to trail across my bed, in any case? And why was its owner locked in silence and immobility? Surely startled innocence would have cried out, questioned my grasp or struggled against it! My captive did neither.

I began to paint a picture against the darkness; the picture of a crouching woman, fear-paralyzed; not daring to stir, to sob or pant or shiver lest she betray herself. Or, perhaps, a woman who was not hushed by panic, but by deliberation. A woman who slowly levelled a weapon, assuring her aim in the blank darkness by such guides as my breathing and the taut direction of her imprisoned tresses. An ugly woman could not have such hair as this. Or, could she? I had a doubtful recollection of various long-haired demonstrators glimpsed in drugshop windows, who were not beautiful. Yes, but they would never have found themselves in such a situation as this one! Only resolve or recklessness could bring a woman to such a pass; and with spirit and this hair no woman could be ugly.

How quiet she was! I suddenly reflected that she must be thinking the same thing of me, since neither of us had moved during a considerable space of time.

Possibly she fancied me only half-aroused, and hoped that I would relapse into sleep without realizing upon what my drowsy grasp had closed. No doubt it would have been the course of chivalry for me to pretend to do so, but it was not the course of curiosity.

The deadlock could not last indefinitely. Apparently, though, it must be I who should break it. As quietly as possible, I brought my left hand forward to grope along that silken line which certainly must guide me to the intruder herself. My hand slipped along the smooth surface to the full reach of my arm; and encountered nothing. Check, for the first attempt! The candle and matches I had bought in the village were also beyond my reach, unless I released my captive and rolled across the bed toward the little bookcase where I had placed them beside the flashlight. If I should speak, what would she do? And—a new thought!—was she alone in the house?

There came a gentle draw at the braid, instantly ceasing as I automatically tightened my hold. The pretense that I slept was ended. I spoke, as soothingly and kindly as I could manage.

"If you will let me strike a light, we can explain to each other. Or, if you will agree not to escape— —?"

In spite of my efforts, my voice boomed startlingly through the dark, still room. No reply followed, but the braid quivered and suddenly relaxed from its tension. She must have come closer to me. Delighted by so much success attained and intrigued by the novelty of the adventure, I moved slightly, stretching my free arm in the direction of the flashlight.

"I am not a difficult person," I essayed encouragement. "Nor too dull, I hope, to understand a mistake or a necessity. Nor am I affiliated with the police! Permit me— —"

I halted abruptly. A cool edge of metal had been laid across the wrist of my groping hand. As the hand came to rest, palm uppermost, I could feel, or imagined I could feel my pulse beating steadily against the menacing pressure of the blade. The warning was eloquent and sufficient; I moved no further toward my flashlight. Of course, if I had lifted my right hand from its guard of the braid, I could easily have pinioned the arm which poised the knife before I suffered much harm. But I might have lost my captive in the attempt; an event for which I was not ready, yet.

"Check," I admitted. "Although, it is rather near a stalemate for us both, isn't it?"

The knife pressed closer, suggestively.

"No," I dissented with the mute argument. "I think not. I do not believe you could do it; not in cold blood, anyway!"

"You do not know," insisted the closer pressing blade, as if with a tongue.

"No, I do not know," I translated aloud. "But I am confident enough to chance it. What reason have you for desperate action? I would not harm you. Have I not a right to curiosity? This is my house, you know. Or perhaps you did not know that?"

A sigh stirred the silence, blending with the ceaseless whisper of the rain that had recommenced through the night. The braid did not move in my right hand, nor did the blade touching my left.

"Speak!" I begged, with an abrupt urgency that surprised myself. "You are the invader. Why? What would you have from me? If I am to let you go, at least speak to me, first! This is—uncanny."

"There is magic in the third time of asking," came a breathed, just audible whisper. "Yet, be warned; call not to you that which you may neither hold nor forbid."

"But I do call—if that will make you speak to me," I returned, my pulses tingling triumph. "Although, as to not holding you——"

"You fancy you hold me? It is not you who are master of this moment, but I who am its mistress."

Her voice had gained in strength; a soft voice, yet not weak, used with a delicate deliberation that gave her speech the effect of being a caprice of her own rather than a result of my compulsion. Yet, I thought, she must be crouched or kneeling beside me, on the floor, held like the Lady of the Beautiful Tresses.

"Still, I doubt if you have the disposition to use your advantage," I began.

"You mean, the cruelty," she corrected me.

"I am from New York," I smiled. "Let me say, the nerve. If you pressed that knife, I might bleed to death, you know."

"Would you hear a story of a woman of my house, and her anger, before you doubt too far?"

"Tell me," I consented; and smiled in the darkness at the transparent plan to distract my attention from that imprisoned braid.

She was silent for so long that I fancied the plan abandoned, perhaps for lack of a tale to tell. Then her voice leaped suddenly out of the blackness that closed us in, speaking always in muted tones, but with a strange, impassioned urgency and force that startled like a cry. The words hurried upon one another like breaking surf.

"See! See! The fire leaps in the chimney; it breathes sparks like a dreadful beast—it is hungry; its red tongues lick for that which they may not yet have. Already its breath is hot upon the wax image on the hearth. But the image is round of limb and sound. Yes, though it is but toy-large, it is perfect and firm! See how it stands in the red shine: the image of a man, cunningly made to show his stalwartness and strength and bravery of velvet and lace! The image of a great man, surely; one high in place and power. One above fear and beyond the reach of hate!

"The woman sits in her low chair, behind the image. The fire-shine is bright in her eyes and in her hair. On either side her hair flows down to the floor; her eyes look on the image and are dreadfully glad. Ha, was not Beauty the lure, and shall it not be the vengeance?

"The nine lamps have been lighted! The feathers have been laid in a circle! The spell has been spoken; the spell of Hai, son of Set, first man to slay man by the Dark Art!

"The man is at the door of the woman's house. Yes, he who came in pride to woo, and proved traitor to the love won—he is at her door in weakness and pain.

"As the wax wastes, the man wastes! As the mannikin is gone, the man dies!

"On her doorstep, he begs for life. He is coward and broken. He suffers and is consumed. He calls to her the love-names they both know. And the woman laughs, and the door is barred.

"The door is barred, but what shall bar out the Enemy who creeps to the nine lamps?

"See, the fire shines through the wax! The image is grown thin and wan. Three days, three nights, it has shrunk before the flames. Three days, three nights, the woman has watched. As the fire is not weary, she is not weary. As the fire is beautiful, she is beautiful.

"The man is borne to her door again. He lifts up his hands and cries to her. But now he begs for death. Now he knows anguish stronger than fear. And the woman laughs, and the door is barred.

"The fire shines on a lump of wax. The man is dead. From her chair the woman has arisen and stands, triumphant.

"But what crouches behind her, unseen? The lamps are cast down! The pentagram is crossed! The Horror takes its own."

The impassioned speech broke off with the effect of a snapped bar of thin metal. In the silence, the steady whisper of rain came to my ears again, continuing patiently. I became aware of a rich yet delicate fragrance in the air I breathed. It was not any perfume I could identify, either as a composition or as a flower scent. If I may hope to be understood it sparkled upon the senses. It produced a thirst for itself, so that the nostrils expanded for it with an eagerness for the new pleasure. I found myself breathing deeply, almost greedily, before answering my prisoner's story.

"'Sister Helen,'" I quoted, as lightly as I could.

"And do you think Rossetti had no truth to base his poem upon?" her quiet voice flowed out of the darkness, seeming scarcely the same speech as the swift, irregular utterance of a moment before. "Do you think that all the traditions and learning of the younger world meant—nothing?"

"Are you asking me to believe in witchcraft and sorcery?"

"I ask nothing."

"Not even to believe that you will press the knife if I refuse to free you?"

"Not even that; now!"

Compunction smote me. Her voice sounded more faint, as if from fatigue or discouragement. It seemed to me that the blade against my wrist had relaxed its menace of pressure and just rested in position. I seemed to read my lady's weariness in the slackened vigilance. Perhaps she was really frightened, now that her brave attempt to lull me into incaution had failed.

"Listen, please," I spoke earnestly. "I am going to set you free. I apologize for keeping you captive so long! But you will admit the provocation to my curiosity? You will forgive me?"

A sigh drifted across the darkness.

"I ask no questions," I urged. "But will you not trust me to make a light and give what help I can? You are welcome to use the house as you please. Or, if you are lost or stormbound, my car is in the old barn and I will drive you anywhere that you say. Let us not spoil our adventure by suspicion. In good faith— —"

I opened my hand, releasing the lovely rope by which I had detained my prisoner. Then, with a quickening pulse, I waited. Would she stay? Would she spring up and escape? Would she thank me, or would she reply with some eccentricity unpredictable as her whim to tell me that tale?

She did none of these things. The braid of hair, freed entirely, continued to lie supinely across my open palm. The coolness of the blade still lightly touched my wrist. She might be debating her course of action, I reflected. Well, I was in no haste to conclude the episode!

When the silence had lasted many moments, however, I began to grow restive. Anxiety tinged my speculations. Suppose she had fainted? Or did she doubt my intentions, and was her quietness that of one on guard? I stirred tentatively.

Two things happened simultaneously with my movement. The braid glided away from me, while the knife slipped from its position and tinkled upon the floor. I started up, perception of the truth seizing my slow wits, and reached for my flashlight.

There was no one in the room except myself. Down my blanket was slipping a severed braid of hair, perhaps a foot in length, jaggedly cut across at the end farthest from my hand. Leaning over, I saw on the floor beside the bed a paper-knife of my own; a sharp, serviceable tool that formed part of my writing kit. Before going to bed, I had taken it from my suitcase to trim a candle-wick, and had left it upon the bookstand.

Now I understood why her voice had sounded more distant than seemed reasonable while I held her beside me. No doubt she had hacked off the detaining braid almost as soon as I grasped it. The knife she had pressed against my wrist to keep me where I lay while she made ready for flight; or amused herself with me. Flight? Say rather that she had leisurely withdrawn! Perhaps she had not even heard my magnanimous speech offering her the freedom that she already possessed. If she had stayed to hear me, probably she had laughed.

Perhaps she was still in the house.

I rose and lighted a candle, under the impulsion of that idea, reserving my flashlight for the search. But there was no one in any of the dusty, sparsely furnished rooms and halls through which I hunted. The ancient locks on doors and windows were fastened as I had left them, although my lady certainly had entered and left at her pleasure. Puzzled and amused, I finally returned to my bedchamber.

There was some difference in that room. I was conscious of the fact as soon as I entered and closed the door behind me. The candle still burned where I had left it, flickering slightly in some current of air. There was no change that the eye could find, no sound except the rain, yet I felt an extreme reluctance to go on even a step from where I stood. What I wanted to do was to tear open the door behind me, to rush out into the hall and slam the door shut between this room and myself.

Why? I looked around me, sending the beam of the flashlight playing over the quiet place. Nothing, of course! I walked over to the bookcase, took up the braid I had left there, and sat down in an old armchair to study my trophy. On principle and by habit I had no intention of being mastered by nerves. It was humiliating to discover that I could be made nervous by the mere fact of being in an unoccupied farmhouse after midnight.

The braid was magnificent. It was as broad as my palm, yet compressed so tightly that it was thick and solid to the touch. If released over someone's shoulders, it would have been a sumptuous cloak, indeed! In what madness of panic had the girl sacrificed this beauty? How she must hate me, now the panic was past! The color, too, was unique, in my experience; a gold as vivid as auburn. Or was it tinged with auburn? As I leaned forward to catch the candle-light, a drift of that fragrance worn by my visitor floated from her braid.

At once I knew what had changed in the room. The air that had been so pure when the house was opened, now was heavy with an odor of damp and mould that had seeped into the atmosphere as moisture will seep through cellar walls. One would have said that the door of some hideous vault had been opened into my bedchamber. This stench struggled, as it were, with the volatile perfume that clung about the braid; so that my senses were thrust back and forth between disgust and delight in the strangest wavering of sensation.

I made the strongest effort to put away the effect this wavering had upon me. I forced myself to sit still and think of normal things; of the men whom I was to see next morning, of the plans I meant to discuss with them.

Useless! The stench was making me ill. A wave of giddiness swept over me, and passed. My heart was beating slowly and heavily. Something in my head pulsed in unison. I felt a frightful depression, that suddenly burst into an attack of fear gripping me like hysteria. I wanted to shriek aloud like a woman, to cover my eyes and run blindly. But at the same time my muscles failed me. Will and strength were arrested like frozen water.

As I sat there, facing the door of the room, I became aware of Something at the window behind my back. Something that pressed against the open window and stared at me with a hideous covetousness beside which the greed of a beast for its prey is a natural, innocent appetite. I felt that Thing's hungry malignance like a soft, dreadful mouth sucking toward me, yet held away from me by some force vaguely based on my own resistance. And I understood how a man may die of horror.

Yet, presently, I turned around. Weak and sick, with dragging effort I turned in my chair and faced the black, uncurtained window where I felt It to be.

Nothing was there, to sight or hearing. I sat still, and combated that which I knew *was* there. In the profound stillness, I heard the wind stir the naked branches of the trees, the flowing water through the fragments of the one-time dam, the sputtering of my candle which needed trimming. Sweat ran down my face and body, drenching me with cold. It crouched against the empty window, staring at me.

After a time, the presence seemed not so close. At last, I seemed to know It was gone. In the gush of that enormous relief my remaining strength was swept away like a swimmer in a torrent and I collapsed half-fainting in my chair.

When I was able, I rose and walked through the house again. Again the rooms showed nothing to my flashlight except dull furniture, walls peeling here and there from long neglect, pictures of no merit and dreary subject. I had expected nothing, and I found nothing.

It was on my way upstairs to my bedroom that a sentence from the invisible lady's story came back to my mind.

"What crouches behind her, unseen? The Horror takes Its own— —"

The bedroom door opened quietly under my hand. The rain had ceased and a freshening breeze came from the west, filling the room with sweet country air. The candle had burned down. While I stood there, the flame flickered out.

After a brief indecision, I made my way to the bed, rolled myself in the blankets, and laid down between the four pineapple-topped posts. This time I kept the flashlight at my hand. But almost at once I slept, and slept heavily far into a bright, windy March morning.

CHAPTER III

"Wide is the seat of the man gentle of speech."

—Instruction of Ke' Gemni.

On the second day after my return to New York, my Aunt Caroline Knox called me up on the telephone.

There are reasons why I always feel myself at a disadvantage with Aunt Caroline. The first of these brings me to a trifling matter that I should have set down before, but which I have made a habit of ignoring so far as possible in both thought and speech. As was Lord Byron, I am slightly lame. I admit that is the only quality in common; still, I like the romantic association. Now, my limp is very slight, and I never have found it interfered much with things I cared to do. In fact, I am otherwise somewhat above the average in strength and vigor. But from my boyhood Aunt Caroline always made a point of alluding to the physical fact as often as possible. She considered that course a healthful discipline.

"My nephew," she was accustomed to introduce me. "Lame since he was seven. Roger, do not scowl! Yes; run over trying to save a pet dog. A mongrel of no value whatever!"

Which would have left some doubt as to whether she referred to poor Tatters or to me, had it not been for her exceeding pride in our family tree.

The second reason for my disadvantage before her, was her utter contempt for my profession as a composer of popular music.

Today her voice came thinly to me across the long-distance wire.

"Your Cousin Phillida has failed in her examinations again," she announced to me, with a species of tragic repose. "In view of her father's intellect and my—er—my family's, her mental status is inexplicable. Although, of course, there is your own case!"

"Why, she is the most educated girl I know," I protested hastily.

"I presume you mean best educated, Roger. Pray do not quite lose your command of language."

I meant exactly what I had said. Phillida has studied since she was three years old, exhaustively and exhaustedly. A vision of her plain, pale little face rose before me when I spoke. It is a burden to be the only child of a professor, particularly for a meek girl.

"She has studied insufficiently," Aunt Caroline pursued. "She is nineteen, and her position at Vassar is deplorable."

"Her health— —" I murmured.

"Would not have hampered her had she given proper attention to athletics! However, I did not call up to hear you defend Phillida in a matter of which you are necessarily ignorant. Her father and I are somewhat better judges, I should suppose, than a young man who is not a student in any true sense of the word and ignores knowledge as a purpose in life. Not that I wish to wound or depreciate you, Roger. There is, I may say, a steadiness of moral character beneath your frivolity of mind and pursuit. If my poor brother had trained you more wisely; if you had been *my* son— —"

"Thank you, Aunt," I acknowledged the benevolent intention, with an inward quailing at the clank of fetters suggested. "Was there something I can do for you?"

"Will you meet Phillida at the Grand Central and bring her home? I cannot have her cross New York alone and take a second train out here. Her father has a lecture this afternoon and I have a club meeting at the house."

"With pleasure, Aunt! What time does her train get in?"

"Half after four. Thank you, Roger. And, she looks on you as an elder brother. I believe an attitude of cool disapproval on your part might impress upon her how she has disappointed the family."

"Leave it to me, Aunt. May I take her to tea, between trains, and get out to your place on the six o'clock express?"

"If you think best. You might advise her seriously over the tea."

"A dash of lemon, as it were," I reflected. "Certainly, Aunt, I could."

"Very well. I am really obliged!"

"The pleasure is mine, Aunt."

But that it was going to be Phillida's, I had already decided. She would need the support of tea and French pastry before facing her home. As for treating her with cool disapproval, I would sooner have spent a year at Vassar myself. It was my intention to meet her with a box of chocolates instead of advice. Phil was not allowed candy, her complexion being under cultivation. On the occasions when we were out together it had been my custom to provide a box of sweets, upon which she browsed luxuriously, bestowing the remnants upon some street child before reaching her home.

From the telephone I turned back to that frivolous pursuit of which my aunt had spoken with such tactfully veiled contempt. She was not softened by the respectable fortune I had made from several successful musical comedies and a number of efforts which my publishers advertise as "high-class parlor pieces for the home." In fact, she felt it to be a grievance that my lightness should be better paid than the Professor's learning. In which she was no doubt right!

Ever since my return from my newly purchased farm in Connecticut, however, I had not been working for money or popular approval, but for my own pleasure.

There was a Work upon which I spent only special hours of delicious leisure and infinite labor. It held all that was forbidden to popular compositions; depth and sorrow and dissonances dearer than harmony. I called it a Symphony Polynesian, and I had spent years in study of barbaric music, instruments and kindred things that this love-child of mine might be more richly clothed by a tone or a fancy. Aunt Caroline had interrupted, this morning, at a very point of achievement toward which I had been working through the usual alternations of enjoyment and exasperation, elevation and dejection that attend most workmen. Pausing only to set my alarm-clock, I hurried into recording what I had found, in the tangible form of paper and ink.

I always set the alarm-clock when I have an engagement, warned by dire experiences.

Aunt Caroline had summoned me about eleven in the morning. When the strident voice of the clock again aroused me, I had just time to dress and reach the Grand Central by half-past four. I recognized that I was hungry, that the vicinity was snowed over with sheets of paper, that the piano keys had acquired another inkstain, and my pipe had charred another black spot on the desk top. Well, it had been a good day; and Phillida's tea would have to be my belated luncheon or early dinner. Even so, it was necessary to make haste.

It was in that haste of making ready that I uncovered the braid of glittering hair which I had brought from Connecticut. I use no exaggeration when I say it glittered. It did; each hair was lustrous with a peculiar, shining vitality, and crinkled slightly along its full length. With a renewed self-reproach at sight of its humbled exile and captivity, I took up the trophy of my one adventure. While I am without much experience, such a quantity seemed unusual. Also, I had not known such a mass of hair could be so soft and supple in the hand. My mother and little sister died before I can remember; and while I have many good friends, I have none intimate enough to educate me in such matters. Perhaps a consciousness of that trifling physical disadvantage of mine has made me prefer a good deal of solitude in my hours at home.

The faint, tenacious yet volatile perfume drifted to my nostrils, as I held the braid. Who could the woman be who brought that costly fragrance into a deserted farmhouse? For so exquisite and unique a fragrance could only be the work of a master perfumer. There was youth in that vigorous hair, coquetry in the individual perfume, panic in her useless sacrifice of the braid I held; yet strangest self-possession in the telling of that fanciful tale of sorcery to me.

On that tale, told dramatically in the dark, I had next morning blamed the weird waking nightmare that I had suffered after her visit. The horror of the night could not endure the strong sun and wind of the March morning that followed. Like *Scrooge*, I analyzed my ghost as a bit of undigested beef or a blot of mustard. Certainly the thing had been actual enough while it lasted, but my reason had thrust it away. That was over, I reflected, as I laid the braid back in the drawer. But surely the lady was not vanished like the nightmare? Surely I should find her in some neighbor's daughter, when my house was finished and I went there for the summer? She could not hide from me, with that bright web about her head whose twin web I held.

It had grown so late that I had to take a taxicab to the Terminal, just halting at a shop long enough to buy a box of the chocolates my cousin preferred. But when I reached the great station and found my way through the swirl of travelers to the track where Phil's train should come in, I was told the express had been delayed.

"Probably half an hour late," the gateman informed me. "Maybe more! Of course, though, she may pull in any time."

Which meant no tea for Phillida; instead, a rush across town to the Pennsylvania station to catch the train for her home. As I could not leave my post lest she arrive in my absence, it also meant nothing to eat for me until we reached Aunt Caroline's hospitality; which was cool and restrained rather than festive.

I foresaw the heavy atmosphere that would brood over all like a cold fog, this evening of Phil's disgraceful return from the scholastic arena. Ascertaining from the gateman that the erring train was certain not to pull in during the next ten minutes, I sought a telephone booth.

"Aunt Caroline, Phil's train is going to be very late, possibly an hour late," I misinformed my kinswoman, when her voice answered me. "I have had nothing to eat since breakfast, and she will be hungry long before we reach your house. May I not take her to dinner here in town?"

"Please do not call your cousin 'Phil'," she rebuked me, and paused to deliberate. "You had no luncheon, you say?"

"None."

"Why not? Were you ill?"

"No; just busy. I forgot lunch. I am beginning to feel it, now. Still, if you wish us to come straight home, do not consider me!"

I knew of old how submission mollified Aunt Caroline. She relented, now.

"Well— —! You are very good, Roger, to save your uncle a trip into the city to meet her. I must not impose upon you. But, a quiet hotel!"

"Certainly, Aunt."

"Phillida does not deserve pampering enjoyment. I am consenting for your sake."

"Thank you, Aunt. I wonder, then, if you would mind if we stopped to see a show that I especially want to look over, for business reasons? We could come out on the theatre express; as we have done before, you remember?"

"Yes, but— —"

"Thank you. I'll take good care of her. Good-bye."

The receiver was still talking when I hung up. There is no other form of conversation so incomparably convenient.

The train arrived within the half-hour. With the inrush of travelers, I sighted Phillida's sober young figure moving along the cement platform. She walked with dejection. Her gray suit represented a compromise between fashion and her mother's opinion of decorum, thus attaining a length and fulness not enough for grace yet too much for jauntiness. Her solemn gray hat was set too squarely upon the pale-brown hair, brushed back from her forehead. Her nice, young-girl's eyes looked out through a pair of shell-rimmed spectacles. She was too thin and too pale to content me.

When she saw me coming toward her, her face brightened and colored quite warmly. She waved her bag with actual abandon and her lagging step quickened to a run.

"Cousin Roger!" she exclaimed breathlessly. "Oh, how good of you to come!"

She gripped my hands in a candid fervor of relief and pleasure.

"I am so glad it is you," she insisted. "I was sorry the train could not be later; I wished, almost, it would never get in—and all the time it was you who were waiting for me!"

"It was, and now you are about to share an orgy," I told her. "I have your mother's permission to take you to dinner, Miss Knox."

"Here? In town? Just us?"

"Yes. And afterward we will take in any show you fancy. How does that strike you?"

She gazed up at me, absorbing the idea and my seriousness. To my dismay, she grew pale again.

"I—I really believe it will keep me from just dying."

I pretended to think that a joke. But I recognized that my little cousin was on the sloping way toward a nervous breakdown.

"No baggage?" I observed. "Good! I hope you did not eat too much luncheon. This will be an early dinner."

She waited to take off the spectacles and put them in her little bag.

"I do not need them except to study, but I didn't dare meet Mother without them," she explained. "No; I could not eat lunch, or breakfast either, Cousin Roger. Nor much dinner last night! Oh, if you knew how I dread—the grind! I should rather run away."

"So we will; for this evening."

"Yes. Where—where were you going to take me?"

We had crossed the great white hall to street level, and a taxicab was rolling up to halt before us. Surprised by the anxiety in the eyes she lifted to mine, I named the staid, quietly fastidious hotel where I usually took her when we were permitted an excursion together.

"Unless you have a choice?" I finished.

"I have." She breathed resolution. "I want to go to a restaurant with a cabaret, instead of going to the theatre. May I? Please, may I? Will you take me where I say, this one time?"

Her earnestness amazed me. I knew what her mother would say. I also knew, or thought I knew that Phillida needed the mental relaxation which comes from having one's own way. In her mood, no one else's way, however, wise or agreeable, will do it all.

"All right," I yielded. "If you will promise me, faith of a gentlewoman, to tell Aunt Caroline that I took you there and you did not know where you were going. My shoulders are broader than yours and have borne the buffeting of thirty-two years instead of nineteen. Had you chosen the place, or shall I?"

To my second surprise, she answered with the name of an uptown place where I never had been, and where I would have decidedly preferred not to take her.

"They have a skating ballet," she urged, as I hesitated. "I know it is wonderful! Please, please— —?"

I gave the direction to the chauffeur and followed my cousin into the cab. It seemed a proper moment to present the chocolates from my overcoat pocket. When she proved too languid to unwrap the box, I was seriously uneasy.

"You cannot possibly know how dreadful it is to be the only child of two intellectual people who expect one to be a credit," she excused her lack of appetite, nervously twitching the gilt cord about the package. "And to be stupid and a disappointment! Yes, as long as I can remember, I have been a disappointment. If only there had been another to divide all those expectations. If only you had been my brother!"

"Heaven forbid!" I exclaimed hastily. "That is— —"

"Don't bother about explaining," she smiled wanly, "I understand. But you are distinguished, and you look it. I never will be, and I am ugly. Mother expects me to be an astronomer like Father and work with him, or to go in for club life and serious writing as she does. I never can do either."

"Neither could I, Phil."

"You are clever, successful. Everybody knows your name. When we are out, and people or an orchestra play your music, Mother always says: 'A trifle of my nephew's, Roger Locke. Very original, is it not? Of course, I do not understand music, but I hear that his last light opera— —' And then she leans back and just *eats up* all the nice things said about your work. She would never let you know it, but she does. And that is the sort of thing she wants from me. I—I want to make cookies, and I love fancywork."

The taxicab drew up with a jerk before the gaudy entrance to Silver Aisles.

I imagine Phillida had the vaguest ideas of what such places were like. When we were settled at a table in a general blaze of pink lights, beside a fountain that ran colored water, I regarded her humorously. But she seemed quite contented with her surroundings, looking about her with an air I can best describe as grave excitement. At this hour, the room was not half filled, and the jazz orchestra had withdrawn to prepare for a hard night's work.

After I had ordered our dinner, I glanced up to see her fingers busied loosening the severe lines of her brushed back hair.

"Everyone here looks so nice," she said wistfully. "I wish my hair did shine and cuddle around my face like those women's does. Do—do I look queer, Cousin? You are looking at me so——?"

"I was thinking what pretty eyes you have."

Her pale face flushed.

"Really?"

"Most truthfully. As for the hair, isn't that a matter of bottled polish and hairdressers? But you remind me of a question for you. Isn't a braid of hair this wide," I laid off the dimensions on the table, "this long, and thick, a good deal for a woman to own?"

"Show me again."

I obeyed, while she leaned forward to observe.

"Not one girl in a hundred has so much," she pronounced judgment. "Who is she? Probably it isn't all her own, anyhow!"

"It is not now, but it was," I said remorsefully.

"How could you tell? Did you measure it?"—with sarcasm. "Do you remember the maxim we used to write in copybooks? 'Measure a thousand times, and cut once?' One has to be cautious!"

"I cut it first, and then measured."

"What? Tell me."

At last she was interested and amused. There was no reason why I should not tell her of my midnight adventure. We never repeated one another's little confidences.

She listened, with many comments and exclamations, to the story of the unseen lady, the legend of the fair witch, the dagger that was a paper-knife by day and the severed tresses. She did not hear of the singular nightmare or hallucination that had been my second visitor. My reason had accounted for the experience and dismissed it. Some other part of myself avoided the memory with that deep, unreasoning sense of horror sometimes left by a morbid dream.

The dinner crowd had flowed in while we ate and talked. A burst of applause aroused me to this fact and the commencement of the first show of the evening. The orchestra had taken their places.

"They will hardly begin with their best act," I remarked, surprised by Phillida's convulsive start and rapt intentness upon the stretch of ice that formed the exhibition floor. "Your ballet on skates probably will come later."

"I did not come to see the ballet," she answered, her voice low.

"No? What, then?"

"A—man I know?"

Once when I was a little fellow, I raced headlong into the low-swinging branch of a tree, the bough striking me across the forehead so that I was bowled over backward amid a shower of apples. I felt a twin sensation, now.

"Here, Phillida?"

"Yes."

"Someone from your home town or your college town?" I essayed a casual tone.

"Neither. He belongs here, and they call him Flying Vere. He—Look! Look, Cousin!"

I turned, and saw that the first performer was upon the ice floor.

He came down the center like a silver-shod Mercury. In the silence, for the orchestra did not accompany his entrance, the faint musical ringing of his skates ran softly with him. My first unwilling recognition of his good looks and athletic grace was followed by an equally reluctant admission of his skill. Reluctant, because my anger and bewilderment were hot against the man. My little cousin, my pathetic, unworldly Phillida—and this cabaret entertainer! At the mere joining of their names my senses revolted. What could they have in common? How had she seen him? Having seen him, it was easy to understand how he had fascinated her inexperience. Only, what was his object?

He had seen us, where we sat. I saw his dark eyes fix upon her and flash some message. Her plain little face irradiated, her fingers unconsciously twisting and wringing her napkin, she leaned forward to watch and answer glance for glance.

I would rather not put into words my thoughts. Yet, I watched his performance. In spite of myself, he held me with his swift, certain skill, his vitality and youth.

He was gone, with the swooping suddenness of his appearance. The jazz music clattered out. Phillida turned back to me and began to speak with a hushed rapture that baffled and infuriated me.

"You understand, Cousin Roger? Now that you have seen him, you do understand? No! Let me talk, please. Let me tell you, if I can. It began last summer, at the school where I was cramming for college work. Oh, how tired I was of study! How tired of it I am, and always shall be! I think that side of me never will get rested. Then, in the woods, I met him. He was stopping at a hotel not far away. I—we——"

I waited for her to go on. Instead, she abruptly spread wide her hands in a gesture of helplessness.

"After all, I cannot tell you. Not even you, Cousin! He—he liked me. He treated me just as a really, truly girl who would have partners at dances and wear fluffy frocks and curl her hair. He thought I was pretty!"

The naïve wonder and triumph of her cry, the challenge in her brown eyes, to my belief, were moving things. I registered some ugly mental comments on the rearing of Phil and the kind of humility that is *not* good for the soul.

"Why not?" I demanded. "Of course!"

She shook her head.

"No. Thank you, but—no! Not pretty, except to him. Only to him, because he loves me."

I do not know what impatience I exclaimed. She checked me, leaning across the table to grasp my hand in both hers.

"Hush! Oh, hush, dear Cousin Roger! For it is quite too late. We were married six months ago; last autumn."

When I could, I asked:

"Married legally, beyond mistake? Were you not under eighteen years old?"

"I was eighteen years and a half. There is no mistake at all. We walked over to the city hall in the nearest town, and took out our license, and were married."

"Very well. I will take you home to your father and mother, now; then see this man, myself. If there is indeed no flaw in the marriage and it cannot be annulled, a divorce must be arranged. Any money I have or expect to have would be a small price to set you free from the miserable business. But the first thing is to get you home. We will start now."

She detained my hand when I would have signalled our waiter. Her eyes, shining and solemn as a small child's, met mine.

"No, Cousin, please! I am not going home any more. At least, not alone. I asked you to bring me here where he is, because I am going to stay with my husband."

"Never," I stated firmly.

"Yes."

"Not if I have to send for your father and take you home by force."

"You cannot. I am of age."

"Phillida, I am responsible for you to your parents tonight. Let me take you home, explain things to them, and then decide your course."

"But that is what I most do not want to do!" she naïvely exclaimed.

"You will not?"

"I'm sorry. No."

"Then I must see the man."

"Not—hurt——?"

I recalled the man we had just seen on the skating floor, with a qualm of quite unreasonable bitterness. That anxiety of Phillida's had a flavor of irony for me.

"Hardly," I returned. "There are fortunately other means of persuasion than physical force."

"Oh! But you cannot persuade him to give me up."

I was silent. At which, being a woman, she grew troubled.

"How could you?" she urged.

"You have had no opportunity of judging what influence money has on some people, Phil."

She laughed out in relief.

"Is that all? Try, Cousin."

"You trust him so much?"

"In everything, forever!"

"Then if I succeed in buying him off, promise me that you will come home with me."

"If he takes money to leave me?"

"Yes."

"I should die. But I will promise if you want me to, because I know it never will happen. Just as I might promise to do anything, when I knew that I never would have to carry it out."

"Very well," I accepted the best I could get. "I will go find him."

"There is no need. He is coming here to our table as soon as he is free."

"I will not have you seen with him in this place."

"But I am going to stay here with him," she said.

Her eyes, the meek eyes of Phillida, defied me. My faint authority was a sham. What could be done, I recognized, must be done through the man.

We sat in silence, after that. Presently, her gaze fixed aslant on me as if to dare my interference, she drew up a thin gold chain that hung about her neck and ended beneath her blouse. From it she unfastened a wedding ring and gravely put the thing on her third finger, the school-girl romanticism of the gesture blended with an air of little-girl naughtiness. She looked more fit for a nursery than for this business.

I could tell from the change in her expression when the man was approaching. I rose, meaning to meet him and turn him aside from our table. But Phillida halted me with one deftly planted question.

"You would not leave me alone in this place, Cousin?"

Certainly I would not leave her alone at a table here; not even alone in appearance while I had my interview with the man close at hand. Yet it seemed impossible to speak before her. She calmly answered my perplexity.

"You must talk to him here, of course. I—want to listen to you both. Indeed, I shall not interfere at all, or be angry or hurt! I know how good you mean to be, dear; only, you do not understand."

I sat down again, perforce. When the man's shadow presently fell across our table, it did not soothe me to see Phil thrust her hand in his, her small face enraptured, her fingers locking about his with a caress plain as a kiss. She said proudly, if tremulously:

"Cousin Roger, this is my husband. Mr. Locke, Ethan dear."

He said nothing. His hesitating movement to offer his hand I chose to ignore. I admit that my spirit rose against him to the point of loathing as he stood there, tall, correct in attire—the focus of admiring glances from other diners—in every way the antithesis of my poor Phillida.

"Sit down," I bade curtly, when he did not speak. "Miss Knox insists that we have our interview here. I should have preferred otherwise, but her presence must not prevent what has to be said."

"It won't prevent anything I want to say, Mr. Locke," he answered.

He spoke with a drawl. Not the drawl of affectation, nor the drawl of South or West so cherished by the romantic, but the slow, deliberate speech of New England's upper coasts. It had the oddest effect, that honest, homely accent on the lips of a performer in this place. Phil drew him down to the third chair at the table. After which, she folded her hands on the edge of the cloth as if to signify to me how she kept her promise of neutrality, and looked fixedly at her glass of water instead of at either of us. Plainly, all action was supposed to proceed from me.

"My cousin has just told me of her marriage," I opened, as dryly concise as I could manage explanation. "It is of course impossible that she should adopt your way of living, as she seems to have in mind. You may not understand, yet, that it also is impossible for you to adopt hers. No doubt you have supposed her to be the daughter of wealthy people, or at least people of whom money could be obtained. You were wrong. Professor Knox has nothing but his modest salary. Her parents are of the scholarly, not of the moneyed class. She has no kin who could or would support her husband or pay largely to be rid of him. Of all her people, I happen to be the best off, financially. It happens also that I am not sentimental, nor alarmed at the idea of newspaper exploitation for either of us. It is necessary that all this be plainly set forth before we go further.

"Now, for your side: you have involved Miss Knox to the extent of marriage. To free her from this trap into which her inexperience has walked is worth a reasonable price. I will pay it. I shall take her home to her father and mother tonight, and consult my lawyer tomorrow. He will conduct negotiations with you. The day Miss Knox is divorced from you without useless scandal or trouble-making, I will pay to you the sum agreed upon with my lawyer. If you prefer to make yourself objectionable, you will get nothing, now or later."

He took it all without a flicker of the eyelids, not interrupting or displaying any affectation of being insulted. I acknowledge, now, that it was an outrageous speech to make to a man of whom I knew nothing. But it was so intended; summing up what I considered an outrageous situation brought about by his playing upon a young girl's ignorance of such fellows as himself. Phillida's usually pale cheeks were burning. Several times she would have broken in upon me with protests, if Vere had not silenced her by the merest glances of warning. A proof of his influence over her which had not inclined me toward gentleness with him!

When I finished there was a pause before he turned his dark eyes to mine, and held them there.

"Honest enough!" he drawled, with that incongruous coast-of-Maine tang to his leisureliness. "I'll match you there, Mr. Locke. I don't care whether you make fifty thousand a year with your music writing, or whether you grind a street-piano with a tin-cup on top. It's nothing to me. I guess we can do without your lawyer, too. Because, you see, I married Mrs. Vere because I wanted her; and I figure on supporting her. If her folks are too cultivated to stand me, I'm sorry. But they won't have to see me. So that's settled!"

He was honest. His glance drove that fact home to me with a fist-like impact. There was nothing I was so poorly prepared to meet.

Phillida's hands went out to him in an impulsive movement. He covered them both with one of his for a moment before gently putting them in her lap with a gesture of reminder toward the revellers all about us. The delicacy of that thought for her was another disclosure of character, unconsciously made. Worthy or unworthy, he did love Phil.

I am not too dully obstinate to recognize a mistake of my own. Whatever my bitterness against the man, I had to accord him some respect. I sat for a while striving to align my forces to attack this new front.

"I don't blame you for thinking what you said, Mr. Locke," his voice presently spoke across my perplexity. "I can see the way things came to you; finding me here, and all! I'm glad to have had this chance to talk it out with one of my wife's relations. I'd like them to know she'll be taken care of. Outside of that, I guess there is nothing we have to say to each other."

"I suppose I owe you both an apology," I said stiffly.

"Oh, that's all right—for both of us! I can see how much store you set by her."

"But what are you going to do with her, man?" I burst forth. "Do you expect to keep her here; sitting at a table in this place and watching you do your turn, making your fellow performers her friends, seeing and learning——?" I checked my outpouring of disgust. "Or do you propose to shut her up in some third-class boarding house day and night while you hang around here? Good heavens, Vere, do you realize what either life would be for an nineteen-year-old girl brought up as she has been?"

He colored.

"As for bringing up," he retorted, "I guess she couldn't be a lot more miserable than her folks worried her into being. But—you're right about the rest. That's why I was going to leave her with her folks yet a while, until I had a place for her. I mean, while I saved up enough to get the place."

"But I wrote to him when I failed in my exams, Cousin Roger," Phillida broke in. "I told him that I would not go home. I could not bear it. I was coming to him, and he would just have to keep me with him or I should *die*. Indeed, I do not care about places. I think it will be lovely fun to sit here and watch him, or go behind the scenes with him and make friends with the other people. I—I am surprised that you are so narrow, Cousin Roger, when all your own best friends are theatrical people and artists and you think so highly of them."

I answered nothing to that. The distance between the stage and this class of cabaret show was not to be traversed in a few seven-league words. I looked at Vere, who returned my look squarely and soberly.

"You needn't worry about her being here, Mr. Locke," he said. "I know better than that! But she has to come to me; it's her right, don't you think? I'll promise you to take her to a better place as soon as I can manage."

"What kind of a place?"

"I'm saving to get a place in the country," he answered diffidently. "I'm a countryman, and Phillida thinks she'd like it."

"You?" I exclaimed, unable to smother my derision and unbelief. My glance summed up his fastidious apparel and grooming, the gloss on his curling dark hair and the dubious diamond on his little finger.

He reddened through his clear, dark skin, but his eyes were not those of a man taken in a lie.

"Did you take notice of what I do here?" He asked me, with the first touch of humility I had seen in him. "I couldn't dance or sing or do parlor tricks. I wasn't bred to parlors or indoors. But I learned to skate pretty fancy from a boy up. My folks' farm was on one side of a lake and the schoolhouse on the other. About November that lake used to freeze solid. My brother and I used to skate five miles to school, and back again, before we were six years old. We lived on skates about half the year, I guess. Well—you don't care about the rest; how the farm was just about big enough to support my elder brother and his family, and I came to New York. Nor how I found New York pretty well filled up with folks who knew considerably more than I did. It was the manager of this place who advertised for expert skaters, who dressed me up like this, and paid me the first living wages I'd had in the city. All the same, I was bred a farmer, and I mean to get back to it. Always have! You're a man, Mr. Locke, and I'd hate you to think I was a shimmy dancer on ice and nothing else, or I wouldn't mention it. My father would have taken the buggy-whip to me, I guess, if he'd lived to see me in this rig. Soon as I've enough put by, I'll shed this perfumed suit and the cheap jewelry and take my wife where she can have a chance to forget I ever wore them."

"But I *like* them," put in Phillida ardently. "Please do not fuss so, Ethan; because I really do."

"Do you?" I turned upon her. "Are you sure, then, that it is not all this cabaret glamour you really are in love with? Would you care for him as an ordinary, hard-working fellow in a pair of overalls and a flannel shirt? No applause, no lights, no stage?"

She laughed up at me.

"You have forgotten that I met Ethan while he was on a vacation from his work here, and roughing it. When I married him, I had hardly seen him in anything except his Navy flannel shirt, scrubby trousers, and funny blunt-toed shoes."

"You served in the war?" I asked him.

He nodded.

"Yes. On a submarine chaser. Got pneumonia from exposure and was invalided home just before the Armistice."

"And you came back here?"

"I came here," he corrected me. "I enlisted from Maine. I was discharged in New York. That was when I couldn't find anything I could do, until this skating trick came along."

I sat thinking for a time; as long thoughts as I could command. The obvious course was to send for Phillida's father. Yet what could that vague and learned gentleman do that I could not? I visioned the Professor standing in this riotous, gaudy restaurant, swinging his eye-glasses by their silk ribbon and peering at Vere in helpless distaste and consternation. It was practically certain that Phil would refuse to go home with him.

What if she did go home? I could picture the scene there, when the truth came out. The mortification of her people, the gossip in the little town, her outcast position among the girls and boys with whom she had grown up—what a martyrdom for a sensitive spirit! Of course, the only possible thing considered by Aunt Caroline would be a prompt divorce.

If Phillida refused to consent to a divorce, how could she live at home as the wife of a man her parents had pronounced unfit to receive? If she yielded and gave up Vere, would she be much better off? An embarrassment to her family, the heroine of a stolen marriage and Reno freedom, what chance of happiness would she have in her conventional circle? Especially as she neither was a beauty nor the dashing type of girl who might make capital of such a reputation. Probably she would bury herself in nunlike seclusion, stay in her room when callers came, and wear a veil when she went out to walk.

Meanwhile, she would break her heart for Vere.

Could matters be any worse if she tried life with him, even if the experiment eventually proved a failure and ended in a divorce instead of beginning there? Might not her parents be spared much they most dreaded, if their friends could be told simply that Phillida had made a love match and was with her husband?

Finally, Phillida was a human creature with the right to manage her own life. Had any of us the right to lay hands upon her existence and mould it to our fancy?

I looked up from my revery to find the eyes of both of them fixed on me as if I held their doom balanced upon my palm. Perhaps, in a sense, I did.

"Phil, will you come home to your father and mother, and consider all this a bit more before you decide?" I asked her.

I thought I knew the answer to this, and I did.

"No, Cousin Roger," she refused firmly. "Please forgive me. I know how kind you mean to be, but—no! I shall stay with Ethan. If ever you love anyone, you will understand."

I accepted the decision. There was no reason why I should think of the woman who had spoken to me across the darkness in a voice of melody and power, or why I should seem to feel again the exquisite, live softness of her braid within my hand. But it was so.

"Very well," I said. "Vere, it is to you, then, as Phillida's husband, that I must address any plans. I do not pretend to like the course she has taken. I do not know what action her parents may take, although I believe they will listen to my advice. Putting all that aside, she refuses to come with me and you agree that she cannot stay here.

"I have just bought a farm in Connecticut, intending to use it as a summer home. There are some alterations and repairs being made, but little is to be changed inside the house and it is in perfectly livable shape. Here is my offer. Take Phillida there, and I will make you manager of the place. I will pay all reasonable expenses of putting the land into proper condition and getting such stock and equipment as you judge best; all expenses and up-keep of the house and whatever salary usually is drawn by such managers of small estates. I shall be there, on and off, but you and Phillida must take charge of everything. I am neither a farmer nor a house-keeper, and do not wish to be either. I bought the place only because New York is too hot to work in during three months of the year, and I hate summer resorts. Keep my room ready, and you will find I disturb you little. Of course, hire what servants are necessary.

"Now, if you make the place self-supporting inside of five years, I will deed the whole thing to you two. To put it better, if you succeed in making the farm pay a living for yourselves, I will make it over to you and withdraw. If you fail—well, I suppose you will be no worse off than you are now!"

They were stricken speechless. Perhaps my attitude had not pointed to such a conclusion of our interview. Phillida told me long afterward that she expected me to bid them good-evening and abandon them forever, as my mildest course; with alternative possibilities such as summoning a policeman and having Vere haled to prison. Seeing their condition, I rose.

"I will stroll about and leave you a chance to talk it over," I declared; although there are few ordeals I dislike more than displaying my limp about such public rooms.

Vere stopped me, rising as I rose.

"No need of that, for us," he answered, facing me across the little table. "About giving us your farm, Mr. Locke, that's for the future! Just now, the manager's job is plenty big enough to thank you for. I wish I could say it better. If you'll stay here with Phillida for ten minutes, until I can get back, I'll be obliged."

"Where are you going?"

"To resign here, and get my outfit into a suitcase."

He had taken up my challenge like a man, at least. There were none of the hesitations and excuses to stay in town that I had half expected. It pleased me that he decided for Phil as well as himself. Some of my ideas about marriage are antiquated, I admit. I nodded to him, and sat down again.

It is unnecessary to record the childish things Phillida tried to say to me, while he was gone.

"I am so happy," was her apology for threatened tears. "I never knew anyone—except Ethan—could be so kind. And—and, will you tell Father and Mother?"

"Yes." I winced, though, at that prospect. "Give me that little bag you carry on your wrist."

She obeyed, wide-eyed.

"You do tote a powder-puff. I did not know whether Aunt Caroline permitted it. Rub it on your nose," I advised, passing the bit of fluff to her.

While she complied, almost like a normally frivolous girl, I used the moment to transfer a few banknotes to the bag, so some need might not find her penniless.

Vere came back in not much more than the promised ten minutes. He had changed to gray street clothes and carried a suitcase. I noted that the diamond had disappeared from his finger and his curly head looked as if it had been held under a water-faucet and vigorously toweled to lessen the brilliantine gloss.

"If you'll tell us where your farm is, Mr. Locke, we'll start," he volunteered.

Phillida looked up at him with eyes of adoring trust.

"I had the porter at the Terminal check my suitcase to be called for. We shall have to get it, dear."

In spite of myself, I smiled at their amazing promptitude. There was both reassurance and pathos in its unconscious youth. All this eagerness pressing forward—where? They did not know, nor I. Certainly we did not dream how strange a goal awaited one of us three, or on what weird, desolate path that traveler's foot was already set.

"You had better go to a good hotel for tonight," I modified their plan. "Tomorrow is time enough to go out to the farm, by daylight. Phil has had enough excitement for one day. I will write full directions for the trip, Vere, on the back of this timetable of the railroad you must take."

They were enchanted with this suggestion. Indeed, they were in a state of mind to have assented if I advised them to sit out on a park bench until morning.

Yet, when I had put them and their scanty luggage into a taxicab, I suffered a bad pang of misgiving. What responsibility was I assuming in letting my little-girl cousin go like this? What did I know of this man, or where he would take her? I think Phillida divined something of my trouble, for she leaned out the door to me and held up her face like a child's to be kissed.

"I am so *happy*," she whispered.

I turned to Vere; who had a long envelope in readiness to put in my hand.

"I guess you might like to have these for a while, Mr. Locke," he said, with one of his slow, straightforward glances.

With which farewells I had to be content, and watch their taxi swing out into the bright-dark flow of traffic where it was lost from my sight. After which, I entered another taxicab by my unromantic self and was driven to that railroad station where I would find a train bound to the college town that was the home of Aunt Caroline and her husband. One always thought of Phil's parents in that order, although the Professor was a moderately distinguished scientist and his spouse merely masterful in her own limited circle.

The envelope Vere had given me contained their marriage certificate, his release from the Navy, and his membership card in the American Legion.

CHAPTER IV

"Fair speech is more rare than the emerald found by slave maidens on the pebbles."

—Ptah-Hotep.

At ten o'clock, next morning, I was summoned from my sleep by the bell of the telephone beside my bed. It was not a pleasant sleep, although I had not returned to my apartment until dawn. Nightmare doubts galloped ruthless hoofs over any repose.

Phillida's voice came over the wire to me like the morning song of a bird.

"Good-morning, Cousin Roger. We are going to take the train in a few moments. But I could not leave New York without telling you how happy I am. Are you—did I wake you up? I was afraid that I might, but Ethan said you would like me to call, even so."

"My dear, it was the kindest thought you ever had," I told her fervently.

"Was it?" she hesitated. "Then—were they pretty dreadful to you at home?"

"Quite!"

"Do you suppose they will *do* anything dreadful about us?"

"No. Nothing."

It did not seem necessary to tell her that Aunt Caroline did not know where the runaways had gone, and was thereby debarred from hasty action. Phillida's father had privately agreed with me in this.

"I am so very happy, Cousin Roger!"

"I am glad, Phil."

"And you will come to the farm soon?"

"Soon," I promised.

So the nightmares of immediate anxiety for her galloped themselves away, routed for that time. Like my gold-fish when their bowl has been unduly shaken, I sank down again into the quieted waters of my little world and absorption in my own affairs. There have been hours when I wondered if I was of more importance than they, as a matter of cosmic fact.

A month passed before I kept my promise to go to the farm in Connecticut.

As a first reason, I wanted to leave my young couple alone for a period of adjustment. Also, I was curious to see how they would handle the business left to them. I held telephone conversations with Phillida, and with various contractors now and then. I sent out the furnishings for my own room. Everything else I purposely left to the experimenters.

There was a second reason, more obscure. I wanted to keep for a while the little mystery of the lady who had come to the farmhouse room in the dark of the night. She was pure romance, a rare incident in a prosaic age. My table had been bare of such delicately spiced morsels, and I relished the savor of this one upon my palate. I was not quite ready to find her in the matter-of-fact daughter of some neighbor, who had sought shelter from the storm in that supposedly empty house and probably mistaken me for a tramp.

Perhaps I was equally reluctant to go back and prove that the adventure was ended, that she had been a bird of passage who had gone on with no thought of return.

With all these delays, and the fact that my work really kept me busy in town, April was verging toward May when I finally saw the last of my luggage put into the car and started on my fifty-mile drive to the house by the lake. I did not take this first visit very seriously, or intend it to be over long. To be a constraint upon the household I had established, or assume a right there, was far from the course I planned. It was not certain Vere and I would be comfortable housemates. But to stay away altogether would have hurt Phillida as much as to stay too long, I considered. Probably a week would be about enough for this time.

So lightly, so ignorantly, I stepped from the first great division of my life into the second; not hearing the closing of the gate through which there was no turning back.

CHAPTER V

"The very room, coz she was in,
Seemed warm from floor to ceilin'."

—THE COURTIN'.

I arrived at noon, when a bright sun set the country air afloat with motes like dust of gold. The place seemed drenched in golden light. Even the young grass had gold in its green, and the lake glittered hot with yellow sparkles.

The house was transformed. The cream-colored stucco that hid its homely walls, deep, arched porches that took the place of the old shallow affairs, scarlet Spanish tiles where bleached shingles had been—all united in giving it the gayest, most modern air imaginable. A gravel drive curved in beneath the new porte-cochère, inviting the wheels of my car to explore. Grass had been put in order, flower-beds laid out. The new dam was up, and the miniature lake no longer suggested a swamp. If the place had appealed to me in its dreary neglect, now it held out its arms to me and laughed an invitation.

As I stepped from my car, I heard running feet and a girl sped around the veranda to meet me. She cast herself into my arms before I fairly realized this was Phillida. A Phillida as new to my eyes as the house! After the first greetings I held her off to analyze the change.

She was tanned and actually rosy. The corners of her once sad little mouth turned up instead of down and developed—I looked twice—yes, developed a dimple. The dull hair I always had seen brushed plainly back, now was parted on one side and fluffed itself across her forehead and about her cheeks with an astonishing effectiveness. She was attired in a China-blue linen frock with a scarlet sash knotted in front quite daringly, for Phillida.

"Why, Phil, how pretty we are!" I admired.

She looked up at me like a praised little girl, and smoothed the sash. I noticed she wore above her wedding ring that "diamond" which once had adorned Vere's finger so distastefully to me. It shone bravely in the sunlight with quite a display of fire. Tracing my gaze, she held out her hand for me to see.

"Yes, it was his, Cousin Roger. Of course, we have not very much money yet, and I do not care about all the engagement rings that ever were thought of. But, I was afraid people up here might notice that I had none and think slightingly of Ethan. So I asked him, and we went to a jeweler, who made it smaller to fit me. It is not a false stone, you know. It is a white topaz, and I love it better than the biggest diamond."

"Then you are still happy?"

"Forever and ever, world without end," she answered solemnly.

We went in.

Sun and sweet wind had worked white magic in the long-closed house. Quaint furniture, no longer dust-grimed but lustrous with cleanliness and polish, had quite a different air. Fresh upholstery in cheerful tints, fresh paper on the walls, good rugs, order and daintiness everywhere changed the interior out of my recognition. Already the atmosphere of home and cheer was established.

"Come see your rooms," Phillida invited, enraptured by my admiration. "They are so pretty!"

She ran up the stairs, around the passage, and ushered me into the room of graceful adventure and grotesque nightmare. I stopped on the threshold.

I had ordered the partition removed between the two chambers on this side, giving me one large room. This, with the little bathroom attached, occupied the entire large frontage of the house. This long, spacious room; floors covered by my Chinese rugs, walls echoing the rugs' smoke-blue, my piano in a bright corner, my special easychairs and writing-table in their due places, welcomed me with such familiar comfort that I could not identify the neglected chamber where I had slept one night in the old bed with the four pineapple-topped posts. The windows were opened, and white curtains with their over-draperies of blue silk were swinging in and out on a fresh breeze where the Horror of my dream had seemed to press itself against the black panes. Decidedly, I must have had a bad attack of indigestion that night!

"See how nice?" Phillida was urging appreciation at my side. "We swung those lovely old hangings from the arch, so they can be drawn across the bedroom end of your room, if you like. Although I do not know why you *should* like, everything is so pretty! Your long Venetian mirror came safely, and all your darling lamps. And—and I hope you like it so well, Cousin Roger, that you will stay here always!"

When she left me alone, I walked to the different windows, contemplating the stretches of lawn dotted with budding apple trees and the lake that lay beyond shining in the sun. Was Phillida's charming wish to become a fact, I wondered? Could this rest and calm hold me content here, where I had meant merely to pause and pass on? I looked at the yellow country road meandering past the lake into unseen distance. Should I ever see my Lady of the Beautiful Tresses come that way, or travel that road to where she lived? If I did meet her, would she forgive me the loss of her braid? There would be a test for the sweetness of her disposition!

When a chiming dinner-gong summoned me downstairs, I found Vere awaiting me beside Phillida. We shook hands, and he made some brief, pleasant speech about their having expected me sooner. If pale, timid Phil had become a surprising butterfly, Vere had taken the reverse progress toward the sober grub. I like him better in outing clothes, although he showed even more the unusual good looks which so unreasonably prejudiced me against him. If he felt any strain in our meeting, his slow, tranquil trick of speech and manner covered it. I hope I did as well! It was then I discovered that his wife's pet name for him fitted like a glove. She called him "Drawls."

The luncheon was good; cooked and served by a middle-aged Swedish woman named Cristina. Afterward, I was conducted into the kitchen by the lady of the house, to view the new fittings and improvements. Most odd and pretty it was to see Phillida in that rôle of housewife, and to watch her pride in Vere and deference to him. Let me record that I never saw the daughter of Aunt Caroline fail in this settled course toward her husband. Whether it was born of revulsion from her mother's hectoring domestic methods, or of consciousness that outsiders might rate Vere below his wife in station and education, so her respect for him must forbid their slight, I do not know. But I never saw her oppose him or speak rudely to him before other people. I suppose they may have had the usual conjugal differings, neither of them being angelic. If so, no outsider ever glimpsed the fact.

We spoke of nothing serious on that first day. They both showed me the various improvements finished or progressing, indoors or out.

We dined as agreeably as we had lunched. Quite early, afterward, I excused myself, and left together the two who were still on their honeymoon.

At the door of my room, I pushed a wall-switch that lighted simultaneously three lamps. In this I had repeated the arrangement used by me for years in my city apartment. I have a demand for light somewhere in my make-up, and no reason for not indulging it. There flashed out of the dusk a large lamp upon my writing-table, a tall floor-lamp beside the piano, and a reading-lamp on a stand beside my bed at the far end of the room. All three were shaded in a smoke-blue and rose-color effect that long since had caught my fancy for night work; the shades inset with imitation semi-precious stones, rough-cut things of sapphire, tourmaline-pink and baroque pearl.

I lay emphasis upon this, to make clear how normal, serene and even familiar in effect was the room into which I came. Yet, as I closed the door behind me and stood in that softly brilliant radiance, a shudder shook me from head to foot with the violence of an electric shock. A sense of suffocation caught at my throat like an unseen hand.

Both sensations were gone in the time of a drawn breath, leaving only astonishment in their wake. Presently I went on with the purpose that had brought me upstairs; lifting a portfolio to the table and beginning to unpack the work which I had been doing in New York. As I laid out the first sheets of music, there drifted to my ears that vague sound from the lake I had heard on my first night visit here, while I stood on the tumble-down porch. The sound that was like the smack of glutinous lips, or some creature drawing itself out of thick, viscid slime. As before, I wondered what movement of the shallow waters could produce that result. Not the tide, now, for the new dam was up and the lake cut off from Long Island Sound. The pouring of the waterfall flowed on as a reminder of that fact.

The sound was not repeated. The dusk outside the windows offered nothing unusual to be seen. I finished my unpacking and sat down at my writing-table.

I am not accustomed to heed time. There never has been anyone to care what hours I kept, and I work best at night. Midnight was long past when I thought of rest.

I declare that I thought of nothing more; not even recalling the vague unease felt on entering the room. A day spent in the fresh air, followed by an evening of hard work and journeyings between the piano and table, had left me utterly weary. When I lay down, it was to sleep at once.

CHAPTER VI

"I have made a story that hath not been heard;
A great feat of arms that hath not been seen!"

— AMENEMHE'ET.

I woke slowly. It seemed that I struggled to wakefulness as a spent swimmer struggles toward shore. Up, up through deep poles of sleep I dragged myself, driven by some dimly sensed necessity. Peril had stolen upon me in my unconsciousness, a stalking beast. I knew that with nightmare certainty. It was as if my soul stood affrighted beside my brain, wailing upon its ally to arouse and stand with it against the menace. And my brain answered, but with infinite difficulty; like a drugged warrior who hears the clang of battle and forces numbed limbs to stir, arise and grasp the sword.

I was awake. Suddenly; the swimmer reaching the surface!

How shall I describe Fear incarnate? The Horror was at the open window opposite the foot of my bed, staring in upon me with slavering covetousness of the prey It watched. I lay there, and felt It seek for me across the darkness with tentacles of evil that groped for some part of me upon which It might lay hold.

The room was still. Between the draperies, the window showed nothing to the eye except a dark square faintly tinged with the night luminance of the sky. There was nothing to see; nothing to hear. But gradually I became aware of a hideous odor of mould and mildew, of must and damp decay that loaded the air with disgust.

I lay there, and opposed the approach of the Thing with all the will of resistance in me. The sweat poured from my whole body, so that I lay as in water and the drenched linen of my sleeping-suit clung coldly to me.

It could not pass the defense of my will. I felt the malevolent fury of Its striving. Like the antennæ of some monstrous insect brushing about my body, I felt Its evil desires wavering about my mental self, examining, searching where It might seize. It had not yet found the weakness It sought. If It did — —?

The sickening, vault-like air I must breathe fought for It. So did the darkness. All this time, or the time that seemed so long, I had no more command of my body than a cataleptic patient. Every ounce of force in me had rushed to support the two warriors of the battle: the brain and will that opposed the clutching menace. But now, as I grew more and more fully awake, out of very loathing and danger I drew determination. Slowly, painfully, I began to free my right arm and hand from this paralysis.

As I advanced in resolution, the Thing seemed to recoil. Inch by inch, I moved my hand across the bed toward my reading-lamp on the stand beside me. In proportion as I moved, the dreadful tentacles drew back and away. A last effort, and the chain was in my fingers. I jerked spasmodically.

Rosy light from the lamp flashed over the room. All the quiet comfort of the place sprang into view as if to reassure me; the piano open as I had left it, the table strewn with my evening's work, each bit of furniture, each drapery or trinket undisturbed.

The Thing was gone. In the hush I heard my panting breath and the tick of my watch on the stand. It was two o'clock in the morning. As I mechanically read the hour, a cock somewhere shrilled its second call before dawn. The Horror had been true to the legendary time of apparitions.

Weak and chilled, I presently made an attempt to rise. But at the movement, a wave of sickness swept through me. The room seemed to rock and swing. I had just time to recognize the grip of faintness before I fell back on the pillow.

Vivifying sweetness was in my nostrils, which expanded avidly for this new air. Perfume that was a tonic, a subtle elixir; that sparkled upon the senses, sank suavely and healingly through me, so that I seemed to draw refreshment with each breath. Reluctantly, I aroused more and more in response to this unusual stimulant; which somehow gave delicious rest yet drew me from it into life.

I could have sworn someone had touched me. With some exclamation on my lips, I started up; to find myself in darkness. The lamps I had left lighted burned no longer.

This time there was no terror in my awakening. No Thing of nightmare pressed against my window-space. The fragrance persisted; the ghastly smell of mould and corruption was gone. But I wanted light for all that! Reaching for the lamp beside me on its stand, I found the little chain. I felt the chain draw in my fingers and heard the click that should have meant light; but no answering brightness sprang up.

Instead, across the dark came a voice; a voice low-pitched, soft without weakness, keen with exultation:

"Victory! Victory! You have no need of light—who conquered in darkness! The Enemy has fled. It has covered the Unspeakable Eyes from the eyes of a man. By the will of a man Its will has been forbidden. It has dragged Itself back to the Barrier and cowers there for this time. Oh, soldier on the dreadful Frontier, be proud, putting off your armor tonight! Be proud, and rest."

Those practical people who are never unnerved by the intangible, may gauge if they can the weirdness of this address following my first experience, and then smile their contempt of me. For I confess to a moment of uncanny chill. The voice was that of the woman who had trailed her braid of hair into my grasp, the night I first slept here. But, how did she know of the Thing's visit to me? I had not spoken nor uttered a cry throughout Its visitation. How could she have knowledge of that silent struggle between It and me, or of my escape so narrowly won. How, unless she too — — ?

I groped for a glass of water left on my stand. I drank, and felt my dry throat relax.

"Who are you?" I asked.

A sigh trembled toward me.

"I am one who stands on the threshold of your beautiful world, as a traveler stands outside a lighted palace, gazing where she may not enter, and feeling the winter about her."

"Do not suppose me quite a superstitious fool," I said bruskly. "You are a woman. The woman who left a very real braid of hair in my hands, not long ago, to save herself from capture!"

"Yes. Yet, I am neither more nor less real than the One which came for you a while since."

"Then my nightmare was real? A thing of flesh and blood, or clever mechanism? You know it. Perhaps you produced it?"

The rush of my angry suspicion dashed in useless heat against her cool melancholy.

"Real? What is real?" she challenged me. "Turn to the sciences that you should understand better than I, and ask. Stretch out your arm. For a million years men have vowed you touch empty air. They saw and felt it empty. But now a child knows air swarms with life. In that thin nothingness, crowd and move the distributors of death, disease, health, vigor—existence itself. The water you have just tasted is pure and clear in the glass? Pure? Each drop is an ocean of inhabitants clean and unclean. I speak commonplaces. But is there no knowledge not yet commonplace? Oh man, with all the unfathomed universe about us, *dare* you pronounce what is real?"

"What is natural," I began.

She interrupted me.

"Doubtless what is not natural cannot and does not exist. Have you, then, measured Nature? He was a great thinker, one of deep knowledge, who compared Man to a child wandering on the shore of a vast ocean and picking up a pebble here and there."

"Of what would you convince me? And, why?"

"Of what? Danger! Why? Would you watch a man enter a jungle where some hideous beast crouched in ambush, while you neither warned nor armed him? I am here to turn you back. I am the native of that country who runs to cry warning to a stranger; to put into his hand the weapon of understanding."

So solemn, so urgent a sincerity was in her voice, that again chill touched me. The clammy dampness of my garments hung on my limbs as a reminder of the Thing, real or unreal, that twice had made Its presence felt beyond denial. Wild as her words might be, their incredible suggestion was matched by my experience. I sought with my eyes for her, before answering. The room was dark, yet the darker bulk of furniture loomed out enough to be distinguishable. No figure was visible, even traced by the direction of her voice. I was certain that any movement to seek her would mean her flight.

"Do you mean that you want me to go away from this place?" I questioned.

The sigh came again, just audibly.

"Yes. Why should you die?"

Was I wrong in fancying the sigh regretful? Did I not hear a wistful reluctance in her tone? Excitement ran along my veins like burning oil on flowing water. The woman hidden in the dark, the association of her voice with the strange, exquisite fragrance I breathed, the thought of beauty in her born of that lovely braid of hair I had seized—all blended in a spell of human magic. I have said I was a man much alone, and a lame man who craved adventure.

"Just now," I said, "you spoke of some victory. You called me—soldier."

"Is it not victory to have driven back the Dark One? Is he not a soldier who, aroused in the night to meet dreadful assault, sets his face to the enemy and battles front to front? Before the Eyes men and women have died or lost reason, or fled across half the world, broken by fear. What are the wars of man with man, compared with a man's battle against the Unknown? I honor you! I salute you! But—soldier alone on the forbidden Frontier, go! Join your fellows in the world alloted to you; live, nor seek to tread where mankind is not sent."

"How can there be wrong in facing a situation that I did not cause?"

"There is no wrong. There is danger."

"What danger?" I persisted.

"Can you ask me?" she retorted with a hint of impatience. "You who have felt Its grope toward your inner spirit?"

I shuddered, remembering the brush of those antennæ, exploring, examining! But I persisted, beyond my every-day nature. Her speech was for me like that liquor distilled from honey that inflamed the Norsemen to war fury.

"You say I came off victor," I reminded her.

"Yes. But can you conquer again, and again, and again? Will you not feel strength fail, health break, madness creep close? Will you not be worn down by the Thing that knows no weariness and fall its prey at last?"

"It will come—often?"

"Until one conquers, It will come."

I forced away a qualm of panic.

"How can you know?" I demanded.

"Ask me not. I do know."

"But, look here!" I argued. "If as you say, this creature was not meant to meet mankind, how can It come after me this way?"

She seemed to pause, finally answering with reluctance:

"Because, two centuries ago one of the race of man here broke through the awful Barrier that rears a wall between human kind and those dark forms of life to which It belongs. For know that a human will to evil can force a breach in that Barrier, which those on the other side never could pass without such aid."

I neither understood nor believed. At least, I told myself that I did not believe her wild, legendary explanation of the nightmare Thing that visited me. I did not want to believe. Neither did I wish to offend her by saying so!

"You will go," she presently mistook my silence for surrender. "You are wise as well as brave. Good go with you! Good walk beside you in that happy world where you live!"

"Wait!" I cried sharply. Her voice had seemed to recede from me, a retreating whisper at the last word. "No! I will not go. I must—I will know more of you. You are no phantom. Who are you? Where—when can I see you in daylight?"

"Never."

"Why not?"

"I came to hold a light before the dreadful path. The warning is given."

"But you will come again?"

"Never."

"What? The Thing will come, and not you?"

"What have I to do with It, who am more helpless before It than you? Go; and give thanks that you may."

"Listen," I commanded, as firmly as I could. "I am not going away from this house without better reason. All this is too sudden and too new to me. If you have more knowledge than I, you have no right to desert me half-convinced of what I should do."

"I can stay no longer."

"Why can you not come again?"

"You plan to trap me," she reproached.

"No. Word of honor! You shall come and go as you please; I will not make a movement toward you."

"Not try—to see me, even?" she hesitated.

"Not even that, if you forbid."

There was a long pause.

"Perhaps——" drifted to me, a faint distant word on the wind that had begun to stir the tree-branches and flutter through my room.

She was gone. There sounded a click whose meaning did not at once strike me, intent as I was upon the girl. Twice I spoke to her, receiving no reply, before judging that I might rise without breaking my promise. Then I recognized the click of a moment before, as that of the electric switch beside my door. No doubt she had turned off my lights at her entrance and now restored them. I pulled the chain of my reading-lamp, and this time light flashed over the room.

I had known no one would be there, and no one was. Yet I was disappointed.

As I drew on my dressing-gown I heard a clock downstairs strike four. Not a breath or a step stirred in the house. The damp freshness of coming dawn crept in my windows, bringing scents of tansy and bitter-sweet from the fields to strive against the unknown fragrance in my room. The melancholy depression of the hour weighed upon me. Beneath the gentle strife of sweet odors, my nostrils seemed to detect a lurking foulness of mould and decay.

I sat down at my desk, to wait beside the lamp for the coming of sunrise.

CHAPTER VII

"For it is well known that Peris and such delicate beings live upon
sweet odours as food; but all evil spirits abominate perfumes."

—Oriental Mythology.

The breakfast bell, or rather Phillida's Chinese chimes, merrily summoned me
to the dining-room; a homely spell to exercise the phantoms of the night.

My little cousin, rosy beyond belief, trim in white middy blouse and blue skirt,
was already in her place behind the coffeepot. Vere sat opposite her at the round
table. They were holding hands across the rolls and bacon and eggs, their glances
interlocked in a shining content that made my solitariness rather drab and dull to
my own contemplation. At my clumsy step the picture dissolved, of course. Vere
rose while Phillida welcomed me to my chair and went into a young housewife's
pretty solicitude about my fruit and hot eggs.

The sun glinted across the table. The very servant had a smiling air of enjoying
the occasion. I never had a more pleasant breakfast. A big brindle cat purred on the
window-sill beside Phillida; no dainty Persian or Angora, but a battered veteran
whose nicked ears and scarred tail proved him a battling cat of ring experience.

"I planned to have a wee white kitten," Phil explained, while putting a saucer
of milk before the feline tough. "One that would wear a ribbon, you know. You
remember, Cousin Roger, how Mother always forbade pets because she believed
animals carry germs? I meant to have a puss, if ever I had a home of my own. This
one just walked into the kitchen on the first day we came here. Ethan said it was
a lucky sign when a cat came to a new home. He gave it the meat out of his sand-
wiches that we had brought for lunch, and it stayed. So I decided to keep it instead
of a kitten. It really is more cat!"

What footing was here for dreary terrors? In a mirror across the room I
glimpsed my own countenance looking quite as usual. No over-night white hairs
appeared; no upstanding look such as the legend gave to Sir Sintram after he met
the Little Master.

After the meal, Vere asked me to walk over to the lake with him.

We strolled through the old orchard toward the dam. This was my side of the
house. In passing, I looked up at the window against which the Thing had seemed
to press Itself with sickening lust for me. Phillida was framed in the open square,
and shook a dustcloth at us by way of greeting and evidence of her busyness.

The wide, shallow lake lay almost without movement, except at the head of the dam. There the water poured over with foam and tumult, an amber-brown cataract some twenty-odd feet across, to rush on below in a winding stream that grew calmer as it flowed.

"We must put our lake in order, Vere," I observed, as we stood on a knoll at the head of the dam. "All this growth of rank vegetation ought to be pulled up, the banks graded and turfed perhaps, the bottom cleaned up. Water-lilies would look better than cat-tails."

To my surprise, he did not assent. Instead, he set his foot on a boulder and rested his arm upon his knee; looking into the clear water.

"Mr. Locke, I just about hate saying what I have to," he told me in his sober, leisurely fashion. "I expect you won't like it; not at all. Well—best said before you get deeper in. I can't see my way to make farming this place pay."

I was bitterly disappointed. Even at the worst estimate of Vere, I had imagined he would stick the thing out a little longer than this. Poor Phillida's time of happiness should have lasted more than these few weeks. But the call of New York, of the "lounge lizard's" ease and unhealthy excitement had won already, it seemed. I said nothing at all. The blow was too sore.

"There are too few acres of arable land, and they're used up," Vere was continuing. "I've seen plenty of impoverished, run-out farms in New England. You could pour money into the soil out of a gold pitcher these five years to come, before it began to pay you back. And then your money might better have been put anywhere in bank, for profit! I saw that, the first week here. Since then I've been looking around for something better to do."

"And have found it, of course," I said bitingly. "Or else you would be drawing your salary as manager and saying nothing to me of all this! Well, where does poor Phil go, and when?"

He turned his dark-curled head and regarded me with calm surprise.

"I didn't exactly know that my wife was going anywhere, Mr. Locke."

"What? You do not mean to leave the farm?"

"Not unless you're tired of our bargain. I've been calculating how to make it pay. That won't be by planting corn and potatoes and taking a wagon-load into town! If you think I'm wrong, call in any practical man who knows this sort of business. We've got to think closer to win here. That's why I'd like to set the lake to work instead of just prettying it up."

"The lake, Vere? There isn't enough water-power over the dam to do any more than run a toy, is there?"

He motioned me nearer to where he stood gazing down.

"Notice what kind of water this is, Mr. Locke? Brown like forest water, sort of green-lighted because the bottom is like turf; neither mud nor sand, but a kind of under-water moss? You see? It's pure and clean, with a little fishy smell about it. Matter of fact, it is forest water! Comes from way off yonder, the stream does, before it spreads out into our lake, here. I borrowed a boat and followed back two miles before it got too shallow for me. Boys have caught trout here three times since I've been watching."

"Well?"

"My father was fish-warden in our district. I learned the business. If you're willing, I can start some trout-raising that ought to pay well. You know, the State is glad to help game preserving, free."

He proceeded to give me a brief lecture on the subject, in his quiet, unpretentious manner; producing notes and diagrams from his pockets. He had written to various authorities and exhibited their replies. He knew exactly what the State would do, what he himself must do, and what investment of money would be required. I listened to him in admiration and astonishment.

From fish raising, he went on to discuss each acre of the farm; its best use in view of its situation, condition, and our needs. We could afford so much labor, it appeared, and no more. We must have certain apparatus; methodically listed with prices. If we used a certain sheltered south field for a peach orchard, the trees planted should be such an age and have giant-powder blast deep beds for them in order that they might soon bear fruit.

When at last he ended his deceptive speech that sounded so lazy while implying so much energy, and turned his black eyes from the papers on his knee to my face, I had been routed long since.

"Vere," I said abruptly, "did you know that I thought you were going to desert the farm, when you began to speak?"

He nodded.

"Yes, I guess so. You don't exactly like me; haven't had any occasion to! You don't judge me a fit match for your cousin. Well, neither would anyone else, yet!"

He began to gather his papers together, his attention divided with them while he finished his answer:

"There will be plenty of time before that 'yet' runs out. Mighty pleasant time, thanks to you, Mr. Locke! Phillida and I expect to enjoy building things up as much as we'll enjoy it after they're all built. Meantime, I prize what you're doing all the more because I know how you feel. Now, if you'd be interested to look over these plans or submit them to someone you've confidence in, for inspection, I'll just turn them over to you."

He had so accurately measured me that I was disconcerted. It was quite true that he was compelling my respect, while my first dislike of him still obstinately lurked in the background of my mind. I felt ungenerous, but I would not lie to him.

"I am a queer fellow, Vere," I said. "Leave that to time, as you say! As for the plans, they are far beyond my scope. A city man, it has been my way to 'phone for an expert when anything was to be done, or to buy what I fancied and pay the bills. In this case, you are the expert. The plans seem brilliant to me. Certainly they are moderate in cost. Keep them, and carry them out as soon as that may be done. You are master here, not I."

We walked back together through the sun and freshness of the early spring morning. As we neared the house Phillida's voice hailed us. She was at my window again, leaning out with her hair wind-ruffled about her face.

"Cousin Roger," she summoned me, "I have found out what makes your room as sweet as a garden of spices. See what it is to be a composer completely surrounded by royalties, able to buy the most gorgeous scents to lay on one's pillow! And all enclosed in antique gold!"

She held up some small object that shone in the sunlight. "Throw it down," I begged, startled into excitement.

She complied, laughing. Vere sprang forward, but I made a quicker step and caught the thing.

It was one of those filigree balls of gold wrought into openwork, about the size of a walnut, that fine ladies used to wear swung from a chain or ribbon and call a pomander. The toy held a chosen perfume or essence supposed to be reviving in case miladi felt a swoon or megrim about to overwhelm her; as ladies did in past centuries and do no longer.

Whose gentle pity had brought this pomander to my pillow, to help me from that faintness which had followed my struggle with the Thing? Whose was the exquisite, individual fragrance contained in the ball I held? I had a vision of a figure, surely light and soft of movement, haloed with such matchless hair as the braid I had captured, stealing step by timid step across my room; within my reach while I lay inert. Perhaps her face had bent near mine in her doubt of my life or death; hidden eyes had studied me in the scanty starlight.

Oh, for Ethan Vere's good looks and athlete's grace, to lure my lady from her masquerade!

"Where did you buy it, Cousin Roger? 'Fess up!" Phillida's merry voice coaxed me.

"It was given to me," I slowly answered. "I cannot offer it to you, Phil. But I will buy any other pretty thing you fancy, instead, next time I go to town."

She made a gesture of disclaim.

"I did not mean *that*! Only, do tell me what the perfume is?"

"I was going to ask if you knew."

"No. Something very expensive and imported, I suppose. Perhaps whoever gave it to you had it made for herself alone, as some wealthy women do. It is the most clinging, yet delicately refreshing scent I ever met."

"Tuberose," suggested Vere.

"Drawls, no. How can you? Like an old-fashioned funeral!" she cried.

"Tuberose didn't always go to funerals," he corrected her teasingly, as she made a face at him. "I remember them growing in my Aunt Bathsheba's garden. Creamy looking posies, kind of kin to a gardenia, seems to me! Thick-petalled, like white plush, and holding their sweet smell everlastingly. But Mr. Locke's perfumery isn't just that, either. There was something else grew in that garden—I can't call to mind what I mean. Basil, maybe?"

"The basil plant, that feeds on dead men's brains," quoted Phil with a mock shiver. "You *are* happy in your ideals, Drawls!"

He laughed.

"Well, that garden smelled pretty fine when the dew was just warming up in the sun, mornings—and so does this little gilt ball! I'll guess Mr. Locke's lady never got it from France. Smells like old New England."

There was no reason why a vague chill should creep over me, or the sunshine seem to darken as if a thin veil drifted between me and the surrounding brightness. Let me say again that no place could have been more unlike the traditional haunted house. There hung about it no sense of morbidity or depression. Yet, what was I to think? I was not sick or mad; and the Thing had come to me twice. I turned from the married lovers and made my way to the veranda, where I might be alone to consider the pomander whose perfume was like a diaphanous presence walking beside me.

Seated there, in one of the deep willow-chairs Phillida had cushioned in peacock chintz and marked especially mine by laying my favorite magazines on its arm, I studied my new trophy of the night. There was a satisfaction in its material solidity. It was real enough, resting in my palm.

Yes; but it was not ordinary among its quaint kind! As I picked out the design of the gold-work, that fact was borne in upon my mind. Here was no pattern of scroll or blossom or cupids and hearts. The small sphere was belted with the signs of the Zodiac, beautiful in minute perfection. All the rest of the globe was covered with lace-fine work repeating one group of characters over and over. I was not learned enough to tell what the characters were, but the whole plainly belonged to those strange, outcast academies of astrology, alchemy—magic, in short. It contained what appeared to be a pinkish ball; originally a scented paste rolled round and dried, I judged by peering through the interstices of the gold.

Had the old-world trinket been left to bewilder me? Why, and by whom? What interest had my lady of the dark in elaborately deceiving me? Why muffle her identity in mystery? Why the indefinable quaintness of language, the choice of words that made her speech so different from even the college-bred Phillida's?

She urged me to leave the house. If she, or anyone associated with her wanted the place left vacant for some reason, why did not the Thing and the warning come to others of our household group? Vere, Phillida, the Swedish woman, Cristina— all had lived here for weeks without any experiences like mine. I had not been told to leave my room, but the house. The danger, then, was only for me?

Well, was I to run away, hands over my eyes, at the first alarm?

The gray cat came purring about me and presently leaped upon my knee.

On impulse, I offered the pomander to its nostrils. The unwinking yellow eyes shut, the beast's powerful claws closed and unclosed with convulsive pleasure, it breathed with that thirsty eagerness for the scent so familiar to my own senses.

"Better than catnip, Bagheera?" I questioned. "You wouldn't bolt from it, either, would you?"

Phillida's battered pet relaxed luxuriously, by way of answer, sniffed toward the hand I withdrew, and composed itself to sleep. I put the pomander in my waistcoat pocket.

I could not deny as mere nightmare the Thing which had visited me. Better confront that fact! It was real. Only, real in what sense? What human agency could produce an effect so frightful, an illusion so hideous that I could scarcely bear to recall it here in full daylight, without the use of a sight or sound to confuse the brain?

Had the girl told the truth in her wild explanation? A truth hinted at by alchemists, Pythagoreans, Rosicrucians, pale students of sorcery and magnificent charlatans, these many centuries? Were there other races between earth and heaven; strange tribes of the middle spaces whose destinies were fixed and complete as our own, but between whose lives and ours were fixed barriers not to be crossed? Had I met one of these beings, inimical to man as a cobra, intelligent as man, hunting Its victim by methods unknown to us?

Was I a cheated fool, or a pioneer on the borders of a new country?

Could I meet that Thing tonight, and tomorrow night? Could I bear the agony of Its presence, the stench of death and corruption that was Its atmosphere? At the mere memory my forehead grew wet.

The postman's buggy had stopped at our mailbox. Phillida ran down to meet the event of the morning. Her laughing chatter came back to me while she waited, fists thrust in middy pockets, for the old man to sort our letters from his bags. It did not appear so hard to make a woman happy, I mused. A man might attempt it with hope, if he could but persuade her to try him.

My lady had promised to come again. Perhaps, with patience— —?

Phillida came across the lawn with an armful of gaudy-covered catalogues and a handful of letters.

"Catalogues for Ethan; letters for you," she called in advance of her arrival. "What an important person you are, Cousin Roger! It always gives me a quivery thrill to realize *who* you are as well as how nice you are. Now, isn't that a jumbled speech to tumble out of me?"

I took her tanned little hand along with the letters; letters that were so many voices summoning me back to pleasant, busy Manhattan.

"It is a fine speech for a humble person to answer, Phil! But does that sort of thing matter to you women? What do you love Vere for, at bottom? Because he is strong and supple and has curly hair? No?" as she shook her head. "Because he has worn the uniform, then; proved his courage in war at sea? Because he had the glamour about him of real adventure and cabaret glitter? Or because he took you away from a life you hated? Or, perhaps, because he is kind and loves you? No! For none of these reasons? Why, then, love Ethan Vere?"

She stopped vigorously shaking her head in repeated denial, and smiled at me triumphantly.

"Because he *is* Ethan Vere," she promptly responded. "Oh, Cousin Roger, you clever people are so stupid! It would not make any difference at all if Drawls were ugly, or never had been a sailor, or could not skate or do things, or had not been able to make me happy. It is something very much bigger than all that!"

"And all the divorce courts, Phil? The breach of promise suits, and the couples who make each other miserable?"

"But they never had anything," she said. "Perhaps they will have it, some day. Don't you know, Cousin Roger, that the most important things in the world are those most people never know about?"

I was not sure whether I knew that, or not. After last night, I was not sure of many things. Still, if such gifts were given as she believed, if it was merely a question of being Ethan Vere—or Roger Locke——?

But I had never seriously considered leaving the adventure.

CHAPTER VIII

"The heart is a small thing, but desireth great matters. It is not sufficient for a kite's dinner, yet the whole world is not sufficient for it."

—HUGO DE ANIMA.

That evening Vere and I settled the business details of the developments he had planned. Also while we three were quietly together, I launched a discussion that had been gathering in my mind all day while I watched Phillida.

"You are doing as efficient work as Vere," I told her. "In fact, you are a most moderate pair! I gave you an open bank account, Phil; and you have furnished the house for so little that I am amazed. And it is all so gay, so freshly pretty! Being an ignorant man, the details are beyond me. But—one servant? Aren't you working yourself too hard? I had expected you to need several. Of course, we are not counting Vere's outdoor force."

She turned in her low chair beside the lamp and glanced toward the window behind her, before replying. I noticed the action, because a moment before Vere had turned precisely the same way.

"It is good of you to think of those things, Cousin Roger," she declared. "But, I want to be a real wife to Drawls. I do, indeed! And I have it all to learn because I was not brought up for that. Look at this dish-towel I am hemming. Cristina would laugh at the stitches if she dared, yet they are better than when I began. Some day I shall sew fine things. So it is with all my housekeeping. I think we should begin as we mean to go on, so I have furnished the house for—us. Perhaps if it had been for you alone, I should have chosen satin-wood and tapestry instead of willow and cretonne. The same way about Cristina. If Ethan and I are to save and earn this lovely place, as you offered, we cannot afford more than one maid. You understand what I am trying to explain, don't you?"

"Yes," I assented. "Surely! What were you looking for, just now, behind you?"

"I? Oh, nothing! I just fancied someone had passed by the window and stared in. I can't imagine what made me fancy that. Unless the cat——" She hesitated.

"Bagheera is asleep under Mr. Locke's chair," Vere observed casually.

"Truly, Cousin Roger, I love the way we are living," she resumed. "It is very miserable of me, I daresay, not to be more intellectual after all Father and Mother labored with me. But it is so! I want to live this way all my life; to be busy, and plan things with Ethan, and make them come true together."

Under cover of the table she put her hand into Vere's, and silence held us a little while. I watched Bagheera the cat, who sat beside my chair staring with unblinking yellow eyes toward the window across the room. Did I imagine a slight uneasiness in those eyes, a wary readiness in gathered limbs and muscles bulking under the old cat's scant fur? Now the tail twitched with a lashing movement.

Presently Bagheera looked away and relaxed. A moment more, and he curled down, composing himself to sleep.

"You like the place, Phil?" I questioned. "You do not find it lonely here, or in any way depressing?"

The candor of her surprise told me that no dweller between the worlds had visited her.

"Cousin Roger? This darling house? Why?"

I passed that question safely, and after a few minutes bade them good-night. They had a fashion of gazing at one another that made it a matter of necessary kindness to leave them alone together.

As I made my solitary way upstairs, I will not deny a growing excitement, or that dread fought with my resolution. Who would keep tryst with me tonight? The Horror or the lady? Both; as each time before? If so, which one would come first, and what might be my measure of success or failure? If some trick were being played upon me, I meant to pluck it out of the mystery.

The quietly pleasant room received me without a hint of the unusual. I lighted the lamps and sat down to my work.

The house was still by ten o'clock, all lights out except mine. At midnight I lay down in the dark, the pomander under my pillow. Whether I put the gold ball there from sentiment, or from some absurd fancy about its perfume and mystic carving being somehow a talisman against evil, or because I feared the trinket might be taken from me during the night, I should be troubled to answer. I did place it there, and lay lapped in its sweet odor while the moments dragged past; heavy, slow-footed moments of strain and dreadful expectation scarcely relieved by a hope uneasy as fear.

The cock crowed for the first hour; and for the second. I slept, at last. When I awoke, level sun-rays were striking across the world.

Nothing had happened.

CHAPTER IX

"These Macedonians are a rude and clownish people that call a
spade a spade."

—PLUTARCH.

Next morning, I took my car and began a systematic investigation of the
neighborhood. There proved to be few houses within reasonable distance where
such a woman as my lady could be lodged. However, I made my cautious inqui-
ries even where the quest seemed useless, resolved to leave no chance untried. No
better plan occurred to me than exhibition of the pomander with a vague story of
wishing to return it to a young lady with red-gold hair. But nowhere did a native
show recognition of the top or the description.

On my way home I overtook a familiar, travel-stained buggy that inspired me
with a fresh disrespect for my own abilities. Why had I not put my question to our
rural mail deliverer in the beginning? Surely here was a man who knew everyone
and went everywhere!

The old white horse rolled placid eyes toward the car that drew up beside it,
then returned to cropping the young grass by the roadside. The postman looked
up from the leather sack open before him, and nodded to me.

"Morning, Mr. Locke," he greeted. "Now let me get the right stuff into this
here box, an' I'll sort your family's right out for you. There's a sample package of
food sworn to make hens lay or kill 'em, for Cliff Brown here, that's gone to the
bottom of the bag. I don't know but Cliff's poultry'd thank me to leave it be! Up
it's got to come, though!"

"Will it make them lay?" I asked, watching the ruddy old face peering into the
sack.

"I guess it might, if Cliff told 'em they'd have to lay or eat it, judgin' from the
smell that sample's put in my bag."

"Not as sweet as this?" I suggested, and leaned across to lay the pomander in
his gnarled hand.

The familiar expression of acute, almost greedy pleasure flowed into his face.
His nostrils expanded with eager intake of the perfume that seemed an elixir of
delight. He said nothing, absorbed in sensation.

"Do you know of a lady who wears that scent?" I asked. "A lady with bright
fair hair, colored like copper-bronze?"

"Not I!" he denied briefly.

"No one at all like that—with hair warmer in shade than ordinary gold color, and a lot of it?"

"No. Not around here, nor anywhere I've been! What do you call this perfumery, Mr. Locke?"

"I have no idea," I answered, sharply disappointed. "No one knows except the young lady I am trying to find. Are you sure you cannot help me at all? There is no newcomer in the neighborhood, no visitor at any house who might be the one I am looking for?"

He shook his head, giving back the pomander with marked reluctance.

"No one who might be able to tell more than yourself?" I persisted.

A gleam of humor lit his eyes. He dropped a cardboard cylinder into Mr. Clifford Brown's mailbox and began to sort out my letters.

"Far as that goes, I guess Mis' Hill don't miss much of what goes on around here. When she hears a good bit of tattle, she has her husband hitch up, and she goes drivin' all day. Ain't a house she knows that don't get to hear the whole yarn! You know Mis' Royal Hill? Mis' Vere gets butter and cheese from her. Might ask her!"

I thanked him and drove on.

Mrs. Hill, garrulous wife of the farmer who owned the place next to ours, was on her porch when I came to a halt before the house. She granted me more interest than the other natives upon whom I had called that morning; inviting me into her parlor to "set," when she had identified me. But she knew nothing of the object of my quest.

"I guessed you must be the new owner up to the Michell place," she observed, her beady, faded brown eyes busy with my appearance, picking up details in avid, darting little glances suggestive of a bird pecking crumbs. "Cliff Brown said a lame feller had bought it. I don't see as that little limp cripples you much, the way you can rampus 'round in that fast automobile of yours! Now, I'm perfectly sound, and I wouldn't be paid to drive the thing. You'd ought to get the other fellow to run it for you; the handsome one. I guess you like to do it, though? Writer, ain't you? Books or newspapers?"

I rallied my scattered faculties to answer the machine-gun attack.

"Music?" she echoed, her narrow, sun-dried face wrinkling into new lines of inquisitiveness. "They said you had a piano in your bedroom, but I thought they were just foolin' me! Seems I never heard of havin' a piano upstairs. Most folks like to show 'em off in the parlor. Must be kind of funny, takin' your company upstairs to play for 'em. But then it's kind of a funny thing for a man to take to, anyhow! I got a niece ten years old next August who can play piano so good there don't seem anythin' left to learn her, so——! But there ain't no use of you drivin' 'round here lookin' for a fair-headed girl, Mr. Locke. The Slav folk down in the shanties by the post road are about the only light-complected ones in this neighborhood. Somehow, we run mostly to plain brown. Senator Allen has two girls, but they're only home from a boardin' school for vacation. How do you like your place?"

"Very much," I assured her. "Only, I do not know a great deal about it, yet. Its history, I mean. Are there any interesting stories about the house? You know, we city people like a nice legend or ghost story to tell our friends when they come to visit us."

She chuckled, swinging in her plush-covered rocking-chair, arms folded on her meagre breast.

"Guess you'll have to make one up! I never heard of none. The Michell family always owned it—and they were so stiff respectable an' upright everyone was scared of 'em! Most of the men were clergymen in their time. The last, Reverend Cotton Mather Michell, went abroad to foreign parts for missionary work with the heathen, twenty-odd years ago; an' died there. He never married, so the family's run out. The Michells were awful hard on women; called 'em vessels of wrath an' beguilers of Adam. Preached it right out of the pulpit—so I guess no girl in these parts could have been hired to wed with him, if he'd wanted. His mother died when he was born, so he'd had no softenin' influence. After news came of his death, the house was shut up 'till you bought it. My, how you've changed it, already! I'd admire to go through it."

When I had invited her to call on Phillida and inspect our domicile, and paid due thanks for information received, she followed me out to the car.

"All this land 'round here is old and full of Indian relics," she remarked. "Over to the Sound where the swamps used to be, there was lots of fightin' with savages. An' they say a witch was stoned to death where the Catholic convent stands now, on the road up above your place. So I guess you can figure out a story to tell your company, if you like."

"A convent?" I repeated, my attention caught by a new possibility. "Do they, perhaps, have visitors there, ladies in retreat for a time, as convents often do abroad?"

Mrs. Hill laughed, shaking her tightly-combed head.

"No hope of your girl there," she chuckled. "They're the strictest sisterhood in America, folks say. Poor Clares, I think they're called. No one, not even their relations, ever see their faces after they join. They're not allowed to talk to each other, even. Just stay in their cells, an' pray, even in the middle of the night, an' shave their heads an' live on a few vegetables an' dry bread."

I laughed with her. Certainly no convent would harbor my lady of marvelous tresses and magical perfume, of wild fancies and heretical theories. That thought of mine was indeed far afield. But where, then, was I next to seek?

I made a detour and used some strategy to gain a view of the Senator's daughters. They proved to be brunettes who wore their locks cropped after the fashion of certain Greenwich villagers. My disappointment was not great; my lady was not suggestive of a boarding-school miss. But I had hoped to find somewhere a trace of the copper-bronze head whose royalty of hair I had shorn as the traitors shore

King Childeric's Gothic locks.

I drove home with a sense of blankness upon me. Suppose she never came again? Suppose the episode was ended? Not even freedom from the Thing could compensate for the baffled adventure.

Think of the lame feller with an Adventure!

CHAPTER X

"Plato expresses four kinds of Mania—Firstly, the musical; secondly, the telestic or mystic; thirdly, the prophetic; and fourthly, that which belongs to Love."

—Preface to Zanoni.

For myself, I have always found that excitement stimulates imagination. There are others, I know, who can do no creative work except when all within and without is lulled and calm. Perhaps I have too much calm as an ordinary thing! That evening, when I went to my room, lighted my lamps and closed my door, I stood alone for awhile breathing the mingled sweetness of the country air and the pomander ball. In that interval, there came to me, complete and whole as a gift thrust into my hand, the melody which an enthusiastic publisher since assured me has reached every ear in America.

As to that extravagant statement, I can only measure by the preposterous amount of money the melody has brought me. Perhaps there is a magic about it. For myself, I cannot hear it—ground on a street-organ, given on the stage, played on a phonograph record or delicately rendered by an orchestra—without feeling again the exaltation and enchantment of that night.

I flung myself down at my writing-table, tossing my former work right and left to make room for this. If it should escape before I could set it down! If the least of those airy cadences should be lost!

At three o'clock in the morning I came back to realization of time and place. The composition was finished; it stood up before me like a flower raised overnight. Eight hours had passed since I sat down to the work, after dinner. I was tired. As I began to draw into a pile the sheets of paper I had covered with notes, weariness gripped me like a hand.

Eight hours? If I had shoveled in a ditch twice that long I could have felt no more exhausted. Yielding to drained fatigue of mind and body, I dropped my head upon the arms I folded upon the table. My hot, strained eyes closed with relief, my stiff fingers relaxed. Rest and content flowed over me; my work was done, and good.

Rest passed into sleep, no doubt.

The sleep could not have been long, for not many hours remained before dawn. When I started awake and lifted my head, I found the room in darkness. A perfume was in the air, and the sense of a presence scarcely more tangible than the perfume. Even in the first dazed moment, I knew my lady had come again.

"Do not rise!" her murmuring voice cautioned me. "Unless you wish me to go?"

"No!"

"I am here because I promised to come. It was not wise of you to ask that of me."

"Then I prefer folly to wisdom," I answered, steadying myself to full wakefulness. "Or, rather, I am not sure that you can decide for me which is which!"

"Why? After all, why? Just—curiosity?"

"You, who speak so learnedly of magic and sorcery," I retorted, smiling under cover of the darkness, "have you never heard of the white magic conjured by a tress of hair, a perfume ball, and a voice sweeter than the perfume? An image of wax does not melt before a witch's fire so easily as a man before these things."

"My hair pleased you?" she questioned naïvely.

"Or so easily as a woman melts before admiration!" I supplemented. "I am delighted to prove you human, mystic lady. Please me? Could anyone fail to be pleased with that most magnificent braid? But how can either you or I forgive the cruelty that took it from its owner? Why did you cut it off?"

"So little of it! And I did not know you, then."

"Little? That braid?"

"It reached below my knee, now it is but little less," she answered with indifference. "We all have such hair."

I gasped. My imagination painted the picture of all that shining richness enwrapping a slim young body. It was fantastic beyond belief to sit there at my desk, beneath my fingers the tools of sober, workaday life, and stare into the dark room that held the reality of my vision. She was there, but I could not rise and find her. She was opposite my eyes, but my promise forbade me to touch the lamp and see her.

"Who are 'we'?" I slowly followed her last sentence.

A sigh answered me. On the silence, a memory floated to me of the story she had told while I held her prisoner that first night:

"The woman sits in her low chair. The fire-shine is bright in her eyes and in her hair. On either side, her hair flows down to the floor."

Yes, by legend young witches had such hair; sylphs, undines and all of the airy race of Lilith. I thrust absurdities away from me and offered a quotation to fill the pause:

> "'I met a lady in the meads'
> 'Full beautiful; a faery's child.'
> 'Her hair was long, her foot was light,'
> 'And her eyes were wild.'"

She did not laugh, or put away the suggestion. When I had decided that she did not mean to reply, and was seeking my mind for new speech to detain her with me, she finally spoke what seemed another quotation:

"'A spirit—one of the invisible inhabitants of this planet, neither departed souls nor angels; concerning whom Josephus and Michael Psellus of Constantinople may be consulted. They are very numerous, and there is no climate or element without one or more.' Have you read the writings of the learned Jew or of the Platonist, you who are so very bold?"

"Neither," I meekly admitted. "But neither ancient gentleman could convince me that you are unhuman."

Her answer was just audible:

"Not I—but, It!"

Now I was silenced, for dreadful and uncanny was that whisper in the dark to a man who had met here in this room What I had met.

"Tell me more of this Thing without a name," I urged, mastering my reluctance to evoke even the idea of what the blood curdled to recall. "Why does It hate me?"

"What can I tell you? Even in your world, does not evil hate good as naturally as good recoils from evil? But this One has another cause also!" She hesitated. "And you yourself? How have you challenged and mocked It this very night? Here, where It glooms, you have dared bring the high joy of the artist who creates? Oh, brave, brave!—he who could await alone the visit of the Unspeakable, in the chamber into which the Loathsome Eyes have looked, and write the music of hope and beauty!"

I started, with a hot rush of surprise and pleasure. She had heard my work. She approved it. More than that, not to her was I the lame fellow who ought to get a better man to drive his car!

"Nor should you, who have two worlds of your own," she added in a lower tone, "doubt the existence of many both dark and bright. Go, then, out of this haunted place where a human madness broke through the Barrier. Be satisfied with the victories you have had. Let the visits of the Dark One fade into mere nightmare; and know I am no more a living woman than Franchina Descartes."

"Who was she?"

"Have you not read that early in the seventeenth century there appeared in Paris the philosopher Descartes, accompanied by the figure of a beautiful woman? She moved, spoke, and seemed life itself; but Descartes declared she was an automaton, a masterpiece of mechanism he himself had made. Yet many refused to believe his story, declaring he had by sorcery compelled a spirit to serve him in this form. He called her Franchina, his daughter."

"And the truth?"

"I have told you all the record tells. She was soon lost. Descartes took her with him upon a journey by sea; when, a storm arising, the superstitious captain of the vessel threw the magic beauty into the Mediterranean."

"Thank you. But, are you fairy or automaton?"

"Do not laugh," she exclaimed with sudden passion. "You know I would say that I have no part in the world of men and women. Not through me shall the ancient dread seize a new life. A little time, now, then the doors will close upon me as the sea closed over Franchina. I will not take with me the memory of a wrong done to you. I shall never come to this house after tonight. If you would give me a happiness, promise me you will leave, too."

I had known we should come to this point. After a moment, I spoke as quietly as I could:

"Tell me your name."

She had not expected that question. I think she might have withheld the answer, given time to reflect. But as it was, she replied docilely as a bidden child:

"Desire Michell."

The name fell quaintly on both hearing and fancy, with a rustle of early New England tradition. Desire! I repeated it inwardly with satisfaction before I answered her.

"Thank you. Now, I, Roger Locke, do promise you, Desire Michell, that I will not leave this house until these matters are plainer to my understanding, whether you go or stay. But if you go and come no more, then I surely shall stay until I find a way to trace you or until the Thing kills me."

"No!"

"Yes."

There was a pause. Then, to my utter dismay, I heard her sobbing through the dark.

"Why do you tempt me?" she reproached. "Is it not hard enough, my duty? For me it is such pleasure to be here—to leave for a while the loneliness and chill of my narrow place! But you, so rich in all things, free and happy—how should it matter to you if a voice in the dark speaks or is silent? Let me go."

Wonder and exulting sense of power filled me.

"I can keep you, then?" I asked.

"I am—so weak."

"Desire Michell, I am as alone as you can be, in my real life. I have gone apart from much that occupies men and women; gaining and losing in different ways. One of the gains is freedom to dispose of myself without grief or loss to anyone, except the perfunctory regret of friends. Will you believe there is no risk that I would not take for a few hours with you? Even with your voice in the dark? Come to me as you can, let us take what time we may, and the chances be mine."

"But that is folly! You do not know. To protect you I must go."

"I refuse the protection. Stay! If there is sorrow in knowing you, I accept it. I understand nothing. I only beg you not to turn me back to the commonplace emptiness of life before I found you. Indeed, I will not be sent away."

"If I yield, you will reproach me some day."

"Never."

"It could only be like this—that we should speak a few times before the gates close upon me."

"What gates?"

"I cannot tell you."

"Very well," I took what the moment would grant me. "That is a bargain. Yet, what safety lies in secrecy between us? If we are to help each other, as I hope, would not plain openness be best? You will tell me no more about yourself? Very well. Tell me something more about the enemy in the dark whom I am to meet. You have hinted that It has a special motive for fixing hate upon me beyond mere malignance toward mankind. What is that motive?"

"Ask me not," she faintly refused me.

"I do ask you. My ignorance of everything concerned is a heavy drawback in this combat. Arm me with a little understanding. What moves It against me?"

The pause following was filled with a sense of difficulty and recoil, her struggle against some terrible reluctance. So painful was that effort, somehow clearly communicated to me, that I was about to devour my curiosity and withdraw the question when her whisper just reached my hearing:

"Jealousy!"

"Jealousy? Of what? For whom?"

"For—me."

The monstrous implication sank slowly into my understanding; then brought me erect, gripping the edge of the table lest I forget restraint and move toward her.

"By what right?" I cried. "By what claim? Desire Michell, what has the Horror to do with you?"

The vehemence and heat of my cry struck a shock through the hushed room distinct as the shattering of crystal. There was no answer, no movement; no rebuke of my movement. I was alone. With that confession she had fled.

My cry had been louder than I knew. Presently I heard a door open. Steps sounded along the hall from the rooms on the opposite side of the house. Someone knocked hesitatingly.

"Are you all right, Mr. Locke?" Vere's voice came through the panels.

I crossed to the door and opened it. He stood at the threshold, an electric torch in his hand.

"We thought you called," he apologized. "I thought maybe you were sick, or wanted something; and no light showed around your door."

I found the wall switch and turned on the lamps. As on the last occasion, she had switched the lights off there, beyond my reach unless I broke my promise not to move about the room while she remained my guest.

"Come in," I invited him. "Much obliged to you and Phillida for looking me up! I had been working late and dropped asleep in my chair, with a nightmare as the result."

It was pleasant to have his normal presence, prosaic in bathrobe and pajamas, in my cheerfully lighted room. His dark eyes glanced toward the music-scrawled papers scattered about, then returned to meet my eyes smilingly.

"We heard some of that work," he admitted. "Phil and I—well, I guess we were guilty of sitting on the stairs to hear you play it over. I never listened to a tune that took hold of me, kind of, like that one. We'd certainly prize hearing all of it together, sometime, if you didn't mind."

The warmth of achievement flowed again in me. I crossed to the piano to assemble the finished sheets, answering him with one of those expressions of thanks artists use to cloak modestly their sleek inward vanity. I was really grateful for this first criticism that soothed me back to the reality of my own world.

Across the top of the uppermost sheet of music, in small, square script quaint as the pomander, was written a quotation strange to me:

"We walk upon the shadows of hills across a level thrown, and pant like climbers."

I did not know that I had read the words aloud until Vere answered them.

"So we do! I guess there is more panting over shadows and less real mountain-climbing done by us humans than most folks would believe. Most roads turn off to easy ways before we reach the hills we make such a fuss about. Who wrote that, Mr. Locke?"

"I don't know," I replied vaguely, intent upon Desire Michell's meaning in leaving this to me.

He nodded, and turned leisurely to go.

"Kind of seems to me as if he must have felt like you did when you wrote that piece tonight," he observed diffidently. "As if trouble did not amount to much, taken right. I'll get back to Phil, now. She might be anxious."

Could that be what Desire had meant me to understand? Was there indeed some quality of courage— —?

That is why my most successful composition from the standpoint of money and popularity went to the publisher under the title, "Shadows of Hills." Of course no one connected the allusion. The general interpretation was best expressed by the cover design of the first printing: a sketch of a mountain-shaded lake on which floated a canoe containing two young persons. I was well pleased to have it so.

But—in what land unknown to man towered the vast mountains in whose shadow I panted and strove? Or was my foot indeed upon the mountain itself?

I did not know. I do not know, now.

CHAPTER XI

"If the Dreamer finds himself in an unknown place, ignorant of the country and the people, let him be aware that such place is to be understood of the Other World."

—Oneirocritica Achmetis.

In the morning I drove down to New York. There were affairs demanding attention. Also, I was pressed by an eagerness to get my over-night work into the hands of the publisher. To be exact, I wanted to put the manuscript out of reach of the Thing at the house. Without reason, I had awakened with that instinct strong within me.

The atmosphere of the city was tonic. Merely driving through the friendly, crowded streets was an exhilaration. The practical employment of the day broomed away fantastic cobwebs. In the evening I turned toward Connecticut with a feeling of leaving home behind me. But I would not stay away from the house for a night, risking that Desire Michell might come and find me missing. She might believe I had been seized by cowardice and deserted. She might never return.

I will not deny that I had lied to her. There was no intention in me of accepting her fleeting visits as the utmost she could give. I meant to snatch her out of darkness and mystery, to set her in the wholesome sunlight where Phillida flitted happily. If I could prevent, those gates of which she vaguely spoke never should close between us. But it was plain that I must tread warily. Once frightened away, how could she be found? Her home, her history, even her face, were unknown to me. Tracing her by a perfume and a tress of hair had been tried, and failed. Of her connection with the Dark Thing I refused to think too deeply. Her connection with me must come first.

It was not until I passed the cottage of Mrs. Hill, glimmering whitely in the starlight, where the road made an angle toward the farm, that I recalled our talk in her "best room."

"The Michell family always owned it. The Reverend Cotton Mather Michell went to foreign parts for missionary work twenty years ago and died there— —"

My lady of the night was Desire Michell. A clue?

"He never married, so the family's run out."

It was damp here in the hollow where the road dipped down. A chill ran coldly over me.

Arrived at the garage which had taken the place of our tumble-down barn, I put the car away as quietly as possible. Ten o'clock had struck as I passed through the last village, and our household was asleep. Moving without unnecessary noise, I crossed to the house. Bagheera, the cat, padded across the porch to meet me and rubbed himself around my legs while I stooped to put the latch-key in the lock.

As the key slid in place, I heard the waterfall over the dam abruptly change the sound of its flow, swelling and accelerating as when a gust of wind hurries a greater volume of water over the brink. But there was no wind. Immediately followed that sound from the lake which I can liken to nothing better than the smack of huge lips unclosing, or the suck of a thick body drawing itself from a bed of mud. The cat thrust himself violently between my feet and pressed against the house-door uttering a whimpering mew of urgency. Startled, I looked in the direction of the lake.

At this distance it showed as a mere expanse of darkness, only the reflection of a star here and there revealing the surface as water. What else could be shown, I rebuked my nerves by querying of them; and turned the key. Bagheera rushed into the hall when the door opened wide enough to admit his body. I followed more sedately and closed the door behind us both.

Now I was not acquainted with Bagheera's night privileges. Did Phillida allow him in the house, or not? After an instant's consideration, I bent and picked him up from his repose on the hall rug. He should spend the night shut in with me, out of mischief yet comfortable. Purring in the curve of my arm, he was carried upstairs without objection on his part. Until we reached my room! On its threshold I felt his body stiffen; his yellow eyes snapped open alertly. Cat antipathy to a strange place, I reflected, amused, as I switched on the lights.

"All right, Bagheera," I spoke soothingly, and put him upon the rug.

He bounded erect, fur bristling, tail lashing from side to side after the fashion of a miniature panther. When I stooped to stroke him, he eluded my hand. In a gliding run, body crouched, ears flattened, he sped toward the doorway, was through it and gone.

Well, I decided, he could not be pursued all through the house. It would be easier to explain him to Phillida next morning. I was tired; pleasantly tired. The day had been filled with the enthusiasm and congratulations of my associates, with conferences and plans for launching the new music via theatres and advertising. It ought to "go big," they assured me. In my optimism of mood, I wondered if I had not already driven off the Dark Thing, since the girl had come to me the night past without It appearing before or afterward. Perhaps, woman-timid, she exaggerated the danger and It had retreated after the second failure to overpower me.

I fell asleep with a tranquil conviction that nothing would disturb my rest this night.

Stillness enveloped me, absolute, desolate. Silence contained me. Yet the thought of another scorched against my understanding in a burning communication of intelligence.

"Man," It commanded, "I am here. Fear!"

And I knew that which was my body did fear to the point of death, but that which was myself stood up in revolt.

"Crouch," It bade. "Crouch, pygmy, and beg. Fear! The blood crawls in the veins, the heart checks, the nerves shrink and wither—man, your life wanes thin and faint. Down—shall your race affront mine?"

My heart did stagger and beat slow. Life crept a sluggish current. But there was another force that stiffened to resistance, and gathered itself to compact strength within me.

"No," my thought refused the dark intelligence. "I am not yours. Command your own, not me."

"Weakling, you have touched that which is mine. Into my path you have dared step. Back—for in my breath you die!"

The air my lungs drew in was foul and poisonous. With more and more difficulty my heart labored. Confused memories came to me of men found dead in their beds in haunted rooms. Would morning find me so? Better that way than to yield to the Thing! Better— —

I struggled erect; or fancied so.

Now I saw myself as one who stood with folded arms fronting a breach in a colossal wall. Huge, immeasurably huge that cliff reared itself beyond the sight and ranged away on either side into unknown distances, dully glistening like gray ice, unbroken save in this place. The gray strand on which I stood was a narrow strip following the foot of the wall. Behind me lay a vast, unmoving ocean banked over with an all-concealing mist. Not a ripple stirred along that weird beach, or a ray changed the fixed gray twilight. And I was afraid, for my danger was not of the common dangers of mankind, but that which freezes the blood of man when he draws near the supernatural; the ancient fear.

I stood there, while sweat poured painfully from me, and fronted my enemy who pressed me hard.

The Thing was at the breach, couched in the great cleft that split the Barrier, darkness within darkness. Unseen, I felt the glare of Its hate beat upon me. From It emanated deathly cold, like the nearness of an iceberg in the night, with an odor of damp and mold.

"Puny earth-dweller, lost here," Its menace breathed, "what keeps you from destruction? For you the circle has not been traced nor the pentagram fixed, for you no law has been thrust down. Trespass is death. Die, then."

Only my will held It from me, and I felt that will reel in sickened bewilderment. I had no strength to answer, only the steadfast instinct to oppose.

The Thing did not pass. There in the breach It ravened for me, thrust Itself toward me, pressed against the thin veil of separation between us. I saw nothing, yet knew where It raised Itself, gigantic in formlessness more dreadful than any shape. Its whispered threats broke against me like an evil surf.

"Man, the prey is mine. Would you challenge me? The woman is mine by the pact of centuries. Save yourself. Escape."

The woman? Startled wonder filled me. Was I then fighting for Desire Michell?

Out of the air I was answered as if her voice had spoken; certainty came to grip me as if with her small hands. She had no help but in me. If I fell, she fell. If I stood firm— —? Exultant resolve flared strong and high within me. My will to protect leaped forward.

The Thing shrank. It dwindled back through the gap in the Barrier. But as It fled, a last venomous message drifted to me:

"Again! And again! Tire but once, pygmy— —!"

I was sitting up in bed in my lighted room, my fingers clutching the chain of the lamp beside me. Was some dark bulk just fading from beyond my window? Or was I still dreaming?

I was trembling with cold, drenched as with water so that my relaxing hand made a wet mark on the table beneath the lamp. This much might have been caused by nightmare. But what sane man had nightmares like these?

When I was able, I rose, changed to dry garments and wrapped myself in a heavy bathrobe. There was an electric coffee service in my room kept for occasions when I worked late into the night. I made strong black coffee now and drank it as near boiling as practicable. Presently the blood again moved warmly in my veins.

Then I knew that the chill in the room was not a delusion of my chilled body. I was warm, yet the air around me remained moist and cold, unlike a summer night. It seemed air strangely thickened and soiled, as pure water may be muddied by the passage of some unclean body. In this atmosphere persisted a fetid smell of mold and decay, warring with the homely scent of coffee and the fragrance of the pomander beneath my pillow.

I was more shaken, more exhausted by this encounter with the unknown than by either of my former experiences. A fact which drove home the grim farewell of my enemy! *Tire but once, pygmy— —!* Desire herself had foretold that the dark Thing would wear me down.

Well, perhaps! But not without fighting for Its victory. At least I would be no supine victim. Already I had forced my way—where? Where was that Barrier before which I had stood? Awe sank coldly through me at memory of that colossal land where I was pygmy indeed, an insolent human intruder upon the unhuman. What other shapes of dread stalked and watched beyond that titanic wall? By what swollen conceit could I hope to win against Them?

I would not consider escape by flight, even if the end had been certain destruction. But my head sank to my hands beneath the weight of a profound depression and discouragement.

It was the hour before dawn, traditionally the worst for man. The hour superstition sets apart for its own, when the life flame burns lowest. At a distance a dog had treed some little wood creature, and bayed monotonously.

There was a weakness at the core of my strength. I waged this combat for the sake of Desire Michell. *But what was she to whom the Thing laid claim by the pact of centuries?*

Darkness began to tinge with light. Pale gray filtered into the dusk with grudging slowness. As day approached I saw that a fog enfolded the house in vapor, stealing into the room in coils and swirls like thin smoke. The lamps looked sickly and dim. I forced away my languor, rose and walked to the nearest window.

Something was moving up the slope from the lake; a dim shape about which the fog clung in steamy billows. My shaken nerves thrilled unpleasantly. What stirred at this empty hour? What should loom so tall?

A moment later the figure was near enough to be distinguished as Ethan Vere, bearing several long fishing-rods over his shoulder.

"Vere!" I hailed him, with mingled relief and utter disgust with myself. "Anything going on so early?"

He looked up at me—I never saw Vere startled—and came on to stop beneath the window. Taking off his cap, he ran his fingers through his black curls, pushing their wetness from his forehead. I noticed how the mists painted him with a spectral pallor.

"Good morning, Mr. Locke," he greeted me. "Just as I've been thinking, there are some big snapping-turtles about the lake and creek. I guessed there'd be some war between them and me before that water was safe for use! One of the fellows dragged a duck under, drowned it and started feeding right before my eyes, just now."

"We will have to get a canoe."

He nodded placid assent.

"That'll look pretty on the lake. Phillida will like it. But I guess I'll keep a homely old flat-bottomed punt out of sight around some corner for work. The other craft goes over too prompt for jobs like mine, and don't hold enough. I'm going to fetch my rifle, now. I'd admire to blow that duck-eater's ugly head off."

"I will get into some clothes and be right with you," I invited myself to the hunt.

"I'd like to have you," he replied with his quaint politeness. There were times when I could visualize Vere's New England mother as if I had known her.

The human interlude had been enough to dispel the black humors of the night. When I was ready to go out, I opened the drawer that held the copper-bronze braid and took it into my hand. How vital with youth its crisp resilience felt in my clasp, I thought; young, too, were its luxuriance and shining color. Nonsense, indeed, to fancy ghostliness here or the passing of musty centuries over the head that had worn this tress! A flood of reassurance rose high in me. Whatever the Thing might be, I would trust the girl Desire Michell. Yes, and for her I would stand fast at that Barrier until victory declared for the enemy or for me. Until It passed me, It should not reach her.

I went downstairs to join Vere. The brightening mist was cool and fresh. There was neither horror nor defeat in the promise of the morning.

CHAPTER XII

"In vain I called on Rest to come and stay.
We were but seated at the festival
Of many covers, when One cried: 'Away!'"

—ROSE GARDEN OF SA'ADI.

Now I entered a time of experiences differing at every point, yet interwoven closely, so that my days might compare to a rope whose strands are of violently contrasted colors. The rope would be inharmonious, startling to the eye, but strong to bind and hold. As I was bound and held!

All day I lived in the wholesome household atmosphere evoked by Vere and Phillida. It is impossible to describe the sunny charm they created about the commonplace. Our gay, simple breakfasts where Phillida presided in crisp middy blouse or flowered smock; where the gray cat sat on the arm of Vere's chair, speculative yellow eye observant of his master's carving, while the Swedish Cristina served us her good food with the spice of an occasional comment on farm or neighborhood events—how perfect a beginning for the day! How stale beside our breeze-swept table was any board at which I had ever sat! I do declare that I have never seen a more winning face than the bright one of my little cousin whom her world had pronounced "plain." Vere and I basked in her sunbeams gratefully.

Afterward, we each had our work. Of the three, Vere was the most industrious; slow, steady and unsparing of himself to a degree that accomplished surprising results. Phillida flitted over the place indoors and out, managing the house, following Vere about, driving to village or town with me on purchasing trips for our supplies. I did rather more of my own work than usual, that summer, and consequently had more of the commercial side to employ me.

A healthy, normal life? Yes—until the hours between midnight and dawn.

I never knew when I laid down at night whether I should sleep until sun and morning overlay the countryside; whether the whispering call of Desire Michell would summon me to an hour more exquisite than reality, less satisfying than a dream, or whether I should leap into consciousness of the Loathsome Eyes fixed coldly malignant upon me while my enemy's inhuman hate groped toward me across the darkness Its presence fouled.

For my two guests kept their promises.

If I speak briefly of the coming of the Thing during this time, I do so because the mind shrinks from past pain. It came again, and again. It craftily used the torture of irregularity in Its coming. For days there might be a respite, then It would haunt me nights in succession until my physical endurance was almost spent.

I have stood before the breach in that Barrier, fighting that nightmare duel, until the place of colossal desolation, last frontier the human race might hope to keep, became as well known to me as a landscape on earth. Yet the effect of the Thing's assaults upon me never lessened. On the contrary, the horror gained in strength. A dreadful familiarity grew between It and me. Communication flowed more readily between us with use. I will not set down, perhaps I dare not set down the intolerable wickedness of Its alternate menaces and offered bribes. Contact with Its intelligence poisoned.

There were nights when It was dumb, when all Its monstrous power concentrated and bore upon me, Its will to destroy locked with my will. My victory was that I lived.

In the shadow, Desire Michell and I drew closer to one another.

How can I tell of a love that grew without sight? So much of the love of romance and history is a matter of flower-petal complexions, heart-consuming eyes, satin lips, and all the form and color that make beauty. How can I make clear a love that grew strong and passionately demanding, knew delicate coquetries of advance and evasion, intimacy of minds like the meeting of eyes in understanding—all in the dark? The blind might comprehend. But the blind have a physical communication we had not; touch has enchantments of its own.

Every night, near midnight, I switched off the lights and waited in the chair at my writing-table, where I was accustomed to work. If she had not come by two o'clock, I learned to know she would not visit me that night. I might sleep in that certainty. A strange tryst I kept there in the dark; listening to the flow of the waterfall from the lake, loud in that dead hour's stillness, or hearing the soft, incessant sounds of insect life awake in trees and fields. If she came—a drift of perfume, a movement slight as a curtain stirred by the wind, then an hour with such a companion as the ancient magician might have drawn out of the air to his nine mystic lamps.

Strange, fantastic tales she told me, spun of fancies luminous and frail as threads of glass. She could not speak without betraying her deep learning in sciences rejected and forgotten by the modern world. Alchemy, astrology, geomancy furnished her speech with allusions blank to my ignorance; which she most gently and politely enlightened when I confessed. I learned that the Green Lion of Paracelsus was not a beast, but a recipe for making gold; that Salamandar's Feather was better known today as asbestos; and that the Emerald Table was by no means an article of furniture. I give these examples merely by way of illustration.

On the other side of the shield held between us, I soon discovered that she knew no more of modern city life than a well-taught child who has never left home. She listened eagerly to accounts of theatres and restaurants. The history of Phillida and Ethan Vere seemed to her more moving and wonderful than any story she could tell me. I was amazed and humbled to find that she rated my ability to make music as a lofty art among the occult sciences.

Of the evil Thing that haunted me, we came to say little. To press her with questions meant to end her visit, I found by experience. When I spoke of that strand between the Barrier and the gray mist-hidden sea, her passion of distress closed all intercourse with the plea that I go away at once, while escape was possible, while life remained mine. So for the most part I curbed my tongue and my consuming curiosity; not from consideration, but of necessity.

One night I asked her how the dark Thing spoke to me, by what medium of communication.

"Spirits of all orders can speak to man in every language, so long as they are face to face," she answered, with a faint surprise at my lack of knowledge. "'*When they turn to man, they come into use of his language and no longer remember their own, but as soon as they turn from man they resume their own language, and forget his.*'

"But they themselves are unaware of this fact, for they utter thought to thought by direct intelligence. So if angel or demon turns his back to you, Roger, you may not make him hear you though you call with great force."

"How do you know that, Desire?"

"But by simple reading! Do not Ennemoser and many writers record it?"

"Have you spoken to such beings, Desire?"

The question was rash, but it escaped me before I could check the impulse. To my relief, she answered without resentment:

"No."

"No? The Thing—the enemy that comes to me has never spoken to you?"

"No."

I was silent in amazement and incredulity. The dark creature claimed her, she declared herself helpless to escape from that dominion into normal life, and yet It never had spoken to her? It spoke to me, a stranger most ignorant, and not to the seeress who was familiar with Its existence and the lore which linked humanity to Its fearful kind?

"You do not believe me," her voice came quietly across my thoughts.

"I believe you, of course," I stammered. "I was only—astonished. You have described It, and the Barrier, so often; from the first night——! I supposed you had seen all I have, and more."

"All you have seen? Now tell me with what eyes you have seen the Barrier and the Far Frontier? The eyes of the body, or that vision by which man sees in a dream and which is to the sight as the speech of spirits is to the hearing?"

"I suppose—with the inner sight."

"Then understand me when I say that I have seen with the eyes of another, by a sight not mine and yet my own."

"You mean," I floundered in vague doubts and jealousy of her human associations of which I knew nothing. "You mean—hypnotism?"

She laughed with half-sad raillery.

"How shall I answer you, Roger? Once upon a time, the jewel called beryl was thought unrivaled as a mirror into which a magician might look to see reflected events taking place at a distance, or reflections of the future. But by and by magicians grew wiser. They found any crystal would serve as well as a beryl. Later still, they found a little water poured in a basin or held in the hollow of the hand showed as true a fantasm. So one wrote: *'There is neither crystallomancy nor hydromancy, but the magick is in the Seer himself.'*"

"Well, Desire?"

"Well, Roger—if to see with the sight of another is hypnotism, then every man who writes a book or tells a good tale is a hypnotist; every historian who makes us see the past is a necromancer."

"You read of the Thing——?"

"No," she replied, after a long pause. "I knew It through sympathy with one who died as I would not have you to die, my friend Roger, of whom I shall think long in that place to which I go presently. Question me no more. When the time comes for you to throw a certain braid of hair and a pomander into the fire——"

"I will never do that!"

"No? Well, you might keep the pomander, which is pure gold engraved with ancient signs and the name of the Shining Dawn, Dahana, in Sanskrit characters. Also the perfume it contains is precious, being blent with the herb vervain which is powerful against evil spirits."

"It is not the pomander that I should keep, nor the pomander that holds the powerful spell."

"You—value the braid so much?"

"I value only one other beauty as highly."

"Yes, Roger?"

"Yes, Desire. And that beauty is she who wore the braid."

Now the darkness in the room was dense. Yet I thought I sensed a movement toward me as airy as the flutter of a bird's wing. The fragrance in the atmosphere eddied as if stirred by her passing. But when I spoke to her again, after a moment's waiting, she had gone.

I am sure no housekeeper was ever more nice in her ideas of neatness than my little Cousin Phillida, and no maid more exact in carrying out orders than Cristina. Nevertheless, automobiles pass on the quietest roads, and my windows are always wide open. There is the fireplace, too, with possibilities of soot. Anyhow, there was a light gray dust overlaying the writing-table on the following morning. And in the dust was a print as if a small hand had rested there, a yard from my chair.

A slim hand it must have been. I judged the palm had been daintily cupped, the fingers slender, smooth and long in proportion to the absurd size of the whole affair. My hand covered it without brushing an outline.

I could not put this souvenir away with the braid and the pomander. But I could put its evidence with their witness of Desire Michell's reality.

CHAPTER XIII

"For may not the divell send to their fantasie, their senses being dulled and as it were asleep, such hills and glistering courts
whereunto he pleaseth to delude them?" whereunto he pleaseth
to delude them?"

— KING JAMES' "DEMONOLOGY."

Now I have to record how I walked into the oldest snare in the world.

Perhaps it was the sense of her near presence brought home to me by her hand-
print on the table so close to where my hand rested; perhaps it was her speech of
presently leaving me to return no more. Or perhaps both these joined in urging on
my determination to learn more of Desire Michell before some unknown bar fell
between us. I only know that I passed into a mood of trapped exasperation at my
helplessness and lack of knowledge. It seemed imperative that I should act to save
us both, act soon and surely; yet inaction was bound upon me by my ignorance.
Who was she? Where did she live? What bond held her subject to the Thing from
the Barrier? What gates were to close between us? Why could she not put her
hand in mine, any night, and let me take her away from this haunted place? Why,
at least, not come to me in the light, and let me see her face to face? I was a man
groping in a labyrinth while outside something precious to him is being stolen.

For the first time I found myself unable to work, unable to share our household life with Phillida and Vere, or to find relaxation in driving about the countryside. Anger against Desire herself stirred at the bottom of my mind; Desire, who
hampered me by the word of honor in which she had netted me so securely.

It was then that my enemy from the unknown places began to whisper of the
book.

I encountered that enemy in a new mood. We did not meet at the breach in
the mighty wall, confronted in death conflict between Its will and mine. Instead,
night after night It crept to my window as at our first meeting. I started awake to
find Its awful presence blackening the starlight where It crouched opposite me, Its
intelligence breathing against mine. As always, my human organism shrank from
Its unhuman neighborhood. Chill and repugnance shook my body, while that part
of me which was not body battled against nightmare paralysis of horror. But now
It did not menace or strive against me. It displayed a dreadful suavity I might liken
to the coiling and uncoiling of those great snakes who are reported to mesmerize
their prey by looping movements and figures melting from change to change in
the Hunger Dance of Kaa.

There was a book that held all I longed to know, It whispered to me. A book telling of the woman! She did not wish me to read, for fear I should grow overwise and make her mine. The book was here, in my house. I might arise and find—if I would be guided by It——!

I thrust the whispers away. How could I trust my enemy? If such a book existed, which seemed improbable, there was a taint of disloyalty to Desire in the thought of reading without her knowledge.

The Thing was not turned away. How could I do harm by learning what she was, unless she had evil to conceal? Did I fear to know the truth? As for the book's existence, I had only to accept guidance from It——?

I persisted in refusal. But the idea of the book followed me through my days like a wizard's familiar dogging me. Where could such a volume be hidden, in what secret nook in wall or floor? How came a book to be written about the girl I supposed young, unknown and set apart from the world? Was I letting slip an opportunity by my fastidious notions of delicacy?

Indecision and curiosity tormented me beyond rest. Phillida and Vere began to consider me with puzzled eyes. Cristina developed a habit of cooking individual dishes of especial succulence and triumphantly setting them before me as a "surprise"; a kindness which of course obliged me to eat whether I was hungry or not. I suspect my little cousin abetted her in this transparent ruse. I pleaded the heat as an excuse for all. We were in late August now. Cicadas sang their dry chant in the fields, where the sun glared down upon Vere's crops and painted him the fine bronze of an Indian. Our lake scarcely stirred under the hot, still air.

It was after a day of such heat, succeeded by a night hardly more cool, that the lights in my room quietly went out. I was sitting at my table, some letters which required answers spread before me while I brooded, pen between my fingers, upon the mystery which had become my life. For the moment I attributed the sudden failure of light to some accident at the powerhouse.

Not for long! The hateful cold that crept like freezing vapor into the room, the foul air of damp and corruption pouring into the scented country atmosphere, the frantic revolt of body and nerves—before I turned my eyes to the window I knew the monster from the Frontier crouched there.

"Weakling!" It taunted me. "Puny from of old, how should you prevail? By your fear, the woman stays mine. Miserable earth-crawler, in whose hand the weapon was laid and who shrinking let it fall unused, the end comes."

"The book?" I gasped, against my better judgment.

"The book was the weapon."

"No, or you would not have offered it to me."

"Coward, believe so. Hug the belief while you may. The offer is past."

Past? A madness of bafflement and frustrated curiosity gripped and shook me.

"I take the offer," I cried in passion and defiance. "If there is such a book, show it to me!"

The Thing was gone. Light quietly filled the lamps—or was it that I had opened my eyes? I gripped the arms of my chair, waiting. For what? I did not know. Only, all the horror I ever had felt in the presence of the Thing was slight compared to the fear that presently began to flow upon me as an icy current. There in the pleasantly lighted room, alone, I sank through depths of dread, down into an abyss of despair, down— —

A long sigh of rising wind passed through the house like a sucked breath of triumph. Windows and doors drew in and out against their frames with a rattling crash, then hung still with unnatural abruptness. Absolute stillness succeeded. I felt a very slight shock, as if the ground at my feet was struck.

I fled from the terror for the first time. Yes, coward at last, deserter from that unseen Frontier's defense, I found myself in the hall outside my room, leaning sick and faint against the wall. Behind me the door shut violently, yet I felt no current of air to move it.

From the other side of the house there sounded the click of latch, then a patter of soft-shod feet. Phillida came hurrying down the hall toward me. She was wrapped in some silky pink-flowered garment. Her short hair stood out around her head like a little girl's well-brushed crop. She presented as endearingly natural a figure, I thought, as any man could seek or imagine. The wisdom of Ethan Vere who had garnered his love here!

"Cousin?" she exclaimed. "The hall light is so dim! You almost frightened me when I glimpsed you standing there. Did the wind wake you, too? I think we are going to have a thunder storm, it is so hot and gusty. I heard poor Bagheera mewing and scratching at the door, so I was just going down to let him in before the rain comes."

"Yes," I achieved. Then, finding my voice secure: "I will let in the cat. Where is Vere?"

"He did not wake up, so I tiptoed out. Why?"

"I do not like to have you going about the house alone at this hour."

Her eyes widened and she laughed outright.

"Why, Cousin Roger! What a funny idea to have about our very own house! I have one of the electric flashlights you bought for us all; see?"

What could I tell her of my vision of her womanly softness and timidity brought to bay by the Thing of horror, down in those empty lower rooms? How did I know It stalked no prey but me? Its clutch was upon Desire Michell. These were Its hours, between midnight and dawn.

"Tramps," I explained evasively. "Give me the light."

But she pattered down the stairs beside me, kimono lifted well above her pink-flowered slippers, one hand on the balustrade. The light glinted in the white topaz that guarded her wedding ring, a richer jewel than any diamond in the sight of one who knew the tender thought with which she had set it there. No! The horror was not for her, clothed in her wholesome goodness as in armor of proof. Surely for such as she the Barrier stood unbreached and strong.

When I opened the front door, Bagheera darted in like a hunted cat. A drift of mist entered with him. Looking out, I saw the night was heavy with a low-hanging fog that scarcely rose to the tree tops; a ground-mist that eddied in smoke-like waves of gray where our light fell upon it. Such mists were common here, yet I shivered and shut it out with relief. While I refastened the lock, Bagheera purred around my ankles, pressing caressingly against me as if thanking me after the manner of cats. I remembered this was not the first time he had shown this anxiety and gratitude for shelter.

"Bagheera does love you," Phillida commented, stooping to pat him. "Isn't it funny, though, that he never will go into your room? He is always petting around you downstairs. When Cristina or I are doing up your quarters, he will follow us right up to the door-sill, but we can't coax him inside. Perhaps he doesn't like that perfume you always have about."

A qualm ran through me, recalling the night I had taken the cat there by force and its frantic escape. But I snapped the key fast and straightened myself with sharp self-contempt. Had I fallen so low as to heed the caprices of a pet cat? Was it not enough that I had fled from my enemy after accepting the knowledge It had striven so long to force upon me?

For I had that knowledge. When I had halted in the passage outside my room, in the moment before Phillida had joined me, there had been squarely set before my mental sight the place to seek the book.

"Phillida, there was a bookcase in this house when it was bought," I said. "I believe it stood in my room before the place was altered. A small stand; I remember putting my candle on its top the first night I slept here. Have you seen it?"

Some tone in my question seemed to touch her expression with surprise as she lifted her eyes to mine; or perhaps it was the hour I chose for the inquiry.

"Oh, yes," she answered readily. "I supposed you had noticed it long ago; I mean, where it stands. The quaintest bit, a genuine antique! And holding the stuffiest collection of old books, too! I believe they may be valuable, out-of-print, early editions. If," her voice faltered wistfully, "if Father ever forgives me for being happy with Ethan, and comes to visit us, he would love every musty old volume. Do you think Mother and he ever will, Cousin Roger?"

"I am sure they will, Phil. Feuds and tragic parents are out of date. They must adjust themselves gradually when they realize Vere is—himself. Before you go upstairs to him, will you tell me where to find that bookcase?"

"Now? Why, of course!"

She led me across the hall to her sewing room. I cannot say that she sewed there very much, but she had chosen that title in preference to boudoir or study as more becoming a housewife. She had assembled here a spinning-wheel from the attic, some samplers, a Hepplewhite sewing-table and chairs discovered about the house. Her canaries' cage hung above a great punch-bowl of flowered ware in which she kept gold-fish. A pipe of Vere's balanced beside the bowl showed that his masculine presence was not excluded.

In a corner stood the bookcase. Phillida pulled the chain of a lamp bright under a shade of peacock chintz, and watched me stoop to look at the faded bindings.

"Thank you, Phil," I said. "It may take some time to find the book I want. You had better hurry back to bed before Vere comes hunting for a missing wife."

"Are you going to stay and hunt for the book tonight, then?"

"Unless you are afraid I shall disturb your canaries?"

She did not laugh. Drawing nearer, she stroked my sleeve with a caressing doubt and remonstrance.

"But you have not been to bed at all, and soon it will be morning! Do you have to write your lovely music at night, Cousin Roger? You have been growing thin and tired, this summer. Are you quite well? You are so good that you should be happy, but—are you?"

"Good, Phil?" I wondered, touched. "Why, how did your lazy, tune-spinning, frivolous cousin get that reputation in this branch of the family?"

"You are so kind," she said simply. "Ethan says so. You know, Cousin Roger, that I was over-educated in my childhood; my brain choked with little, little stupid knowledge that hardly matters at all. We went to church Sundays because that was the correct thing to do. But I was almost a heathen when Ethan married me. He doesn't trouble about church. He doesn't trouble about the past, or life after death, or punishment for sin. He believes if one tries to be kind and straight, the big Kindness and Straightness takes care of everything. So I have learned to feel that way, too. It is a—a calm sort of feeling all the time, if you know what I mean. And that is the way you are good, although perhaps you never thought of it."

"Thank you, Phillida," I acknowledged; and walked with her to the foot of the stairs.

When her pink-clad figure had vanished behind her bedroom door, I went back to the sewing room and drew up a chair before the case of books.

Phillida had not unreasonably stigmatized them as stuffy. They were a sober collection. Burton's "Anatomy of Melancholy," an ancient copy of the Apocrypha, and a three-volume Life of Martin Luther loaded the first shelf. I looked at the second shelf and found it filled with the bound sermons of a divine of whom I had never heard.

The lowest shelf held strange companions for the sedate volumes above. Erudite works on theosophy, magic, the interpretation of dreams and demonology huddled together here. Not all of them were readable by my humble store of learning. There was a Latin copy of Artemidorus, Mesmer's "Shepherd," Mathew Paris, some volumes in Greek, and some I judged to be Arabian and Hebrew. At the end of the row stood a thin, dingy book whose title had passed out of legibility. I took it out and opened the covers.

Fronting the first page was a faded woodcut, the portrait of a woman. Beneath in old long-s type, dim on the yellowed paper, was printed the legend:

"Desire Michell, ye foul^e witch."

Closing the book, I forced reason to come forward. I was resolved that panic should not drive me again nor my defense fall from within its walls. Master of my enemy I might never be; master of my own inner kingdom I must and should be. But I was glad to be here instead of upstairs while I read; glad of the interlude in Phillida's company, and of the presence of the three sleepy canaries who blinked down at the disturbing lamp.

The date stamped into the back of the book in Roman numerals was of a year in the seventeen hundreds. What connection could its Desire Michell have with the girl I knew? Perhaps she had adopted the name to mystify me. Or at most, she might be of the family of that unfortunate woman branded witch by a bigoted generation.

Reopening the book, I studied the dim, stiff portrait. The face was young, delicate of line, with long eyes set wide apart; eyes that even in this wretched picture kept a curious drowsy watchfulness. The inevitable white Puritan cap was worn, but curls clustered about the brow and two massive braids descended over either shoulder. The perfumed bronze-colored braid up in my drawer— —?

The volume was entitled "Some Manifestations of Satan in Witchcraft in Ye Colonies," by Abimelech Fetherstone. Disregarding the satanic manifestations set forth in the other four chronicles, I turned to "Ye Foul^e Witch, Desire Michell."

As I began to read, another breath of wind sighed through the house, sucking windows and doors in and out with the shock of sound, instantly ended, that is produced by a distant explosion. I thought a flash of lightning whipped across my eyes. But when I glanced toward the windows I saw only the smoke-like fog banked in drifts against the panes.

CHAPTER XIV

"Beauty is a witch—"

—Much Ado About Nothing.

I will tear the core out of many yellow pages of diffuse writing spiced with smug moral reflections.

Desire Michell had been no traditional old hag, hideous and malevolent; no pallid, raving epileptic to accuse herself in shrieking tales of Black Men, and Sabbats, and harm done to neighbors' cattle or crops. Her father was a clergyman who brought his goods and his motherless daughter from England to the Colonies, and settled in "ye Pequot Marsh country." There he found a congregation, and they lived much respected. Their culture appeared to be far beyond that of their few, hard-working neighbors. Young Mistress Michell was reputed learned in the use of simples, among other arts, and to have been "of a beauty exceeding the custom among godly women, to so great degree that sorcery should have been suspected of her."

However, sorcery was not suspected; not even when her fame spread among near-dwelling Indian tribes who gave her a name signifying *Water on which the Sun is Shining*. Admiration was her portion, then, with all the suitors the vicinity held. But from fastidiousness or ambition she refused every proposal made to her father for her. She walked aloof and alone, until another sort of wooer came to the gate of the minister's house.

This man's full name was not given, apparently through the writer's cautious respect for place and influence. He was vaguely described as goodly in appearance, of high family, but not abundantly supplied with riches. However he chanced to come to the obscure settlement was not stated. He did come, saw Desire Michell, and fell as abjectly prostrate before her as any youth who never had left the village.

He pressed his courtship hard and eagerly. At first he was welcome at the minister's house. But a day came when Master Michell forbade him to cross that door and rumor whispered, scandalized, that Sir Austin's suit had not been honorable to the maid.

Sir Austin sulked a week at the village inn. Then he broke under the torment of not seeing Desire Michell. Their betrothal was made public, and he rode away to prepare his home for their marriage in the spring.

Travel was slow in the winter, news trickled slowly across snowbound distances. With spring came no bridegroom; instead word arrived of his affair with an heiress recently come to New York from England. She was rich in gold and grants of land from the Crown. Her husband would be a man of weight and influence, it seemed.

Sir Austin had married her.

Desire Michell shut herself in her father's house. The clergyman did not live many months after the humiliation. Alone, the girl lived. "Student," wrote Abimelech Fetherstone, "of black and bitter arts. Or as some say, having, like Bombastus de Hohenheim, a devil's bird enchained to do her will."

In his distant home, Sir Austin sickened. He burned with fever, anguish consumed him. Physicians were called to the bedside of the rich man. They could not diagnose his ailment or help him. He screamed for water. When it was brought, his throat locked and he could not swallow. He raved of Desire Michell, beseeching her mercy. In his times of sanity, he begged and commanded his wife and servants to send for the girl. In her pardon he saw his sole hope of life.

Finally, he was obeyed. Messengers were sent to the village. They were not even admitted to the house they sought, or to sight of Mistress Michell.

"Your master came himself to woo; let him come himself to plead."

That was the answer they received to carry back to the sick man.

Sir Austin heard, and submitted with trembling hope. Writhing in the anguish wasting him by day and night, he made the journey by coach and litter to Desire Michell's house. At her door-sill he implored entrance and pity. The door did not open.

It never opened for him. For three days in succession he was borne to her threshold, calling on her in his pain and fear. His servants and physician clustered about staring at the house which stood locked and blank of response. At night fire-shine was seen from an upper room; some declared they heard wild, melodious laughter.

On the third day Sir Austin died. A stern-faced deputation of men went to the house of the late clergymen. They found the door unlatched and open to their entrance. In the upper room they found Mistress Michell seated before her hearth where a dying fire fell to embers, her hair "flowing down in grate bewty."

"What have I to do with Sir Austin, or he with me?" she calmly asked the men who gaped upon her. "How should I have harmed him, who came not near him, as ye know? Bury him, and leave me in peace."

If she had been aged and ugly, she might have been hung. Gossip ran rife through the countryside. But indignation was strong against the man who had jilted the local beauty, there existed no proof of harm done, and the matter slept for a time.

New matters came. A horror grew up around the house. The girl was seen flitting across the fields at dawn, a monstrous shadow following. Her voice was heard from the room where she locked herself alone, raised in unknown speech. Strange lights moved in her windows in the deep night. The old woman who had served in the house for years was stricken with a palsy and was taken away mumbling unintelligible things that iced the blood of superstitious hearers.

There was a young man of the neighborhood whose love for Mistress Michell had been long and constant. One morning he was found dead on her doorstep, his face fixed in drawn terror. Under his hand four words were scrawled in the snow: "*Sara daughter of Ruel — —*"

There were those who could finish that quotation. Next Sabbath the new minister took as his text: "Ye shall not suffer a witch to live." And he spoke of Sara the daughter of Ruel, who was wed to ten bridegrooms, each of whom was dead on the wedding eve; for she was beloved by an evil spirit that suffered none to come to her. Authority moved at last against Desire Michell. But when the officers came to arrest her, she was found dead in her favorite seat before the hearth.

"Fair and upright in her place, scented with a perfume she herself distilled of her learning in such matters; which was said to contain a rare herb of Jerusalem called Lady's Rose, resembling spikenard, with vervain and cedar and secret simples; in which she steeped her hair so that wherever she abode were sweet odours. So did she escape Justice, but shall not escape Hell's Damnation and Heaven's casting out."

I closed the book and laid it down.

Reading those dim, closely printed pages had taken time. I was astonished to find the window spaces gray with dawn, when I glanced that way. The night was past. Neither from Desire nor from the Thing without a name which had sent me to this book could I find out what I was expected to glean from the narration.

My enemy had made no conditions on directing me to the book. It had asked no price, uttered no menace. Why, then, had I so solemn a certainty that a crisis in our affair had been reached. I had come to an end; a corner had been turned. I had opened a door that could not be closed. How did I know this? Why?

Why was the fog against the windows this morning so like the fog that shrouded the unearthly sea opposite the Barrier?

By and by Cristina came downstairs and busied herself in the kitchen. Bagheera, who had slept beside my chair all night, rose and padded out to the region of breakfast and saucers of milk. Next, the voices of Phillida and Vere drifted from above.

To have Phillida find me there in her sewing-room, finishing an all-night vigil, involved too many explanations. I did an unwise thing. From the lowest shelf of the bookcase I gathered such books as were readable by my knowledge, and carried the armful up to my room. After a hot bath and breakfast I would look over these companions of the New England witch book.

CHAPTER XV

"Not a drop of her blood was human,
But she was made like a soft sweet woman."

—LILITH.

The fog stayed all day. The mist was so dense that it gave the effect of a solid mass enclosing the house. No wind stirred it, no cheering beam of sun pierced it. Through it sounds reached the ear distorted and magnified. All day I sat in my room reading.

There are books which should not be preserved. I, who am a lover of books, who detest any form of censorship, I do seriously set down my belief that there exist chronicles which would be better destroyed. With this few people will agree. My answer to them is simple: they have not read the books I mean.

Not all the volumes from the old bookcase were of that character, of course. Nearly all of them were well known to classical students, at least by name. Obscure, fantastic, cast aside by the world they were, but harmless to a fairly steady head. But there were two that clung to the mind like pitch. I have no intention of giving their titles.

Ugly and sullen, early night closed in when I was in a mood akin to it. Dinner with Phillida and Vere was an ordeal hurried through. We were out of touch. I felt remote from them; fenced apart by a heavy sense of guilt and defilement left by those hateful books, most incongruously blended with contempt for my companions' childish light-heartedness. As soon as possible, I left them.

Alone in my room, in my chair behind the writing-table again, I pushed aside the pile of books and sank into sombre thought. What should I say to Desire Michell if she came tonight?

Who was she, who was claimed by the Unspeakable and who did not deny Its claim? Was I confronted with two beings from places unknown to normal humanity? If she was the woman that she had seemed to be throughout our intercourse, how could the dark enemy control her? Even I, a common man with full measure of mankind's common faults and weaknesses, could hold Its clutch from me by right of the law that protects each in his place.

Was she one of those who have stepped from the permitted places?

"*Sara the daughter of Ruel—who was beloved by an evil spirit who suffered none to come to her.*"

"*There was a young gentlewoman of excellent beauty, daughter of a nobleman of Mar, who loved a foule monstrous thing verie horrible to behold, and for it refused rich marriages.... Until the Gospel of St. John being said suddenlie the wicked spirit flue his waies with sore noise."*

I put out my hand and thrust the pile of books aside from my direct sight. But I could not so easily thrust from my mind the thoughts these books had implanted. I could not forget that Desire Michell herself had alleged jealousy as the Thing's reason for attacking me.

What if we came to an explanation tonight and ended this long delirium? Was it not time? Had not my weeks of endurance earned me this right? Resolution mounted in me, defiant and strong.

The evening had passed to an hour when I might look for the girl to come. I switched off the lights, and sat down to keep our nightly tryst.

In the darkness of the haunted room, the thoughts I would have held at bay rushed upon me as clamorous besiegers.

Desire! Desire of the world! Desire of mine and of the unhuman Thing, did we grasp at Eve or Lilith? At the fire on the hearth or the cold phosphorescence of swamp and marsh?

A drift of fragrance was afloat on the air. A delicate stir of movement passed by me. I raised my head from my hands, expectant.

"I am here," her familiar voice told me.

"Desire, you had to come, tonight."

Some quality in my voice carried to her a message beyond the words. But she did not break into exclamation or question as another woman might. She was mute, as one who stands still to find the path before taking a step.

"You are angry," she said at last. "Something here has gone badly for you; I knew that before I entered this room."

"How can you say that?" I challenged. "If you are like other men and women, how can you know what happens when you are absent? How do you know what passes between the Thing from the Frontier and me?"

"I do not know unless you tell me, Roger. If I feel from afar when you are in sorrow, why, so do many people feel with another in sympathy."

"You feel more than ordinary sympathy can," I retorted.

"Then, perhaps it is not an ordinary sympathy I have for you, Roger."

Her very gentleness struck wrong on my perverted mood. Was she trying to turn me from my purpose with her soft speech? She had never granted me anything so near an admission of love until now.

"It is not an ordinary trial that I have borne for these meagre meetings where I do not see your face or touch your hand," I answered. "But that must end. Put your hand in mine, Desire, and come with me. Let us go out of this room where shadows make our thoughts sickly. You shall stay with my cousin. Or if you choose, we will go straight to New York or Boston. I am asking you to be my wife. Let us have done with phantoms and spectres. I love you."

"No," she whispered. "You do not love me tonight. Tonight you distrust me. Why?"

"Is it distrusting you to ask you to marry me?"

"Not this way would you have asked that of me when I last came! But I will answer you more honestly than you do me. To go with you would be the greatest happiness the world could give. To think of it dazzles the heart. But it is not for me. Have you forgotten, Roger, that my life is not mine? That I am a prisoner who has crept out for a little while? The gates soon close, now, upon me."

"What gates?" I demanded.

"Sacrifice and expiation."

"Expiation of what?" I exclaimed, exasperated. "Desire, I have read the book of Desire Michell, downstairs."

I heard her gasp and shrink in the darkness. Silence bound us both. In the hush, it seemed to me that the house suddenly trembled as it had done the night before, a slight shock as from some distant explosion. In my intentness upon the woman opposite me the tremor passed unheeded. She must answer me now, surely! Now— —

She spoke with a breathless difficulty, spacing her words apart:

"How did you—find—the book?"

"It told me—the Thing from out there," I admitted, sullenly defiant of her opinion.

She cried out sharply.

"You? You took Its gift? You did that fatal madness—and you are here? Oh, you are lost, and the guilt mine! Yet I warned you that danger flowed from knowing me. You accepted the risk and the sorrow—yet you have thrown down all for a bribe of knowledge. Do you not know what it means to take a gift from the Dark Ones of the Borderland? To brave the Loathesome Eyes so long—and fall this way at last! Yet—there may be a hope—since you still live. But go. Not tomorrow, not at dawn, but go now. By all that man can dread for soul or body, go now."

"Not without you."

"Me? Oh, how can I make you understand! I shall never come here again. Take with you my gratitude for our hours together, my prayers for all the years to come. There is no blame to you because you could not trust a woman on whom falls the shadow of the awful Watcher that stalks behind me. I make no reproach—if only you will go. Do not linger. I do most solemnly warn you not to stay alone in this room one moment after I have gone."

"Desire!" I exclaimed. "Wait. Forgive me. I trust you. I did not mean what you believe. Do not leave me this way. Desire— —"

I can say honestly that my next action was without intention. On my table lay, as usual, a small electric torch. Every member of our household was provided with one for use in emergencies likely to occur in a country house, the time of candles being past. Now, rising in agitation and repentance, my hand pressed by chance upon the flashlight's button. A beam of light poured across the darkness.

What did I see, starting out of the black gloom? A spirit or a woman? Were those a woman's draperies or part of the night fog that showed mere swirl upon swirl of pale gray twisting in the path of light? I glimpsed a face colorless as pearl, the shine of eyes dark and almond shaped, then a drifting mass of gray smoke, all intermingled with glittering gold flashes, seemed to close between us. The whole apparition sank down out of vision, as aghast, I lifted my hand and the torch went out.

Shaken out of all ability to speak, I stood in my place. Did I hear a movement, or only a stirring of the orchard trees beyond the windows?

"Desire?" I ventured, my voice hoarse to my ears.

No answer. I felt myself alone.

I would not at once turn on the lamps. My haste might seem an attempt to break faith with her a second time. I sat down again, folding my arms upon the table and resting my forehead upon them.

Well, I had seen her at last—but how? A wan loveliness seemingly painted upon the canvas of the dark by a brush dipped in moonlight. A white moth caught fluttering in the ray of the torch. Seen at the instant of her leaving me forever; insulted by my suspicions, my love hurled coarsely at her like a command, my promise of security for her visits apparently broken. How dared I even hope for her return?

Now I knew why my enemy had guided me to those books, that I might read, fill my mind with the poison of vile thoughts, and destroy the comradeship that bound me to Desire Michell. How should I find her? How free us both?

The clock in the hall downstairs struck a single bell. With dull surprise I realized that considerable time had passed while I sat there. Still I did not move, weighed down by a profound discouragement.

Suddenly, as a wave will run up a beach in advance of the incoming tide, impelled by some deep stir in the ocean's secret places, an icy surge rushed about my feet. Deathly cold from that current struck through my whole body. My heart shuddered and staggered in its beating from pure shock.

"Go! Not tomorrow, not at dawn, but now!"

The wave seeped back, receded away from me down its invisible beach. Desire's warning hammered at my mind, striving to burst some barred door to reach the consciousness within that had loitered too long. This was the new peril. This was what I had fled from, unknowing the source of my panic, the night before.

This was death.

A second surge struck me with the heavy shock of a veritable wave from some bitter ocean. This time the tide rose to my knees; boiling and hissing in its rush. Blood and nerves seemed to freeze. I felt my heart stop, then reel on like a broken thing. Flecks of crimson spattered like foam against my eyelids.

The wave broke. The mass poured down the beach, tugging at me in its retreat. With the last strength ebbing away from me with that receding current, I dragged the chain of the lamp beside me.

The comfort of light springing up in the room! The relief of seeing normal, pleasant surroundings! Truly light is an elixir of courage to man.

That cold had paralyzed me. I had no force to rise. Nor did I altogether wish to rise and go. I had lost Desire tonight. Was I to lose my self-respect also? Was I to run a beaten man from this peril, after standing against my enemy so long?

Should I not rather stand on this my ground where I was not the "lame feller"?

Down by the lake, the snarling cry of a terrified cat broke the night stillness. It was Bagheera's voice. The cry was followed by sounds indicating a small animal's frantic flight through the thickets of goldenrod and willow that edged the banks of the stream below the dam. The series of progressive crashes passed back of the house and continued on, dying away down the creek.

As I braced my startled nerves after this outbreak of noise, the light was withdrawn from every lamp in the room. At the same moment, the electric torch rolled off my table and fell to the floor. I heard its progress across the muffling softness of the rug, across the polished wood beyond, and final stoppage at some point out of my reach.

As vapor rises from some unseen source and forms in vague growing mass within the curdled air, so blackening dark the hideous bulk reared Itself in the night and stared in upon me. As so many times, I felt the Eyes I could not see; the pressure of a colossal hate loomed over me, poised to crush, yet withheld by a force greater than either of us. The venom of Its malevolence flowed into the atmosphere about me, fouling the breath I drew. My lungs labored.

"Pygmy," Its intelligence thrust against mine. "Frail and presumptuous Will that has dared oppose mine, you are conquered. This is the hour foretold to you, the hour of your weakness and my strength. Weakling, feel the death surf break upon you. Fall down before me. Cower—plead!"

Now indeed I felt a sickness of self-doubt, for the wash of the invisible sea never had come to me until tonight. And there was Desire's saying that I had destroyed myself by accepting the Thing's gift of knowledge of the book. But I summoned my forces.

"Never," my thought refused It. "Have we not met front to front these many nights? And who has drawn back, Breaker of the Law? You return, but I live. The duel is not lost."

"It is lost, Man, and to me. Have you not taken my gift that you might spy meanly on the secret of your beloved? Have you not opened your mind to the evil thoughts that creep upon the citadel of strength within and tear down its power? Of your own deed, you are mine. My breath drinks your breath. Your life falls down as a lamp that is thrown from its pedestal. Your spirit rises from its seat and looks toward those spaces where it shall take flight tonight. Man, you die."

Again the surge and shock of that frigid sea rushed upon me. I felt the swirl and hiss of the broken wave higher about me before it sank away down whatever dreadful strand it owned. My life ebbed with it, draining low. My enemy spoke the truth. One more such wave— —

My imagination sprang ahead of the event. In fancy, I saw bright dawn filling this room of mine, shining on the figure of a man who had been myself. His head rested on his folded arms so that his face was hidden. On the table beside him a vase was overturned; a spray of heliotrope lay near and water had trickled over scattered sheets of music, staining the paper. By and by Vere would come to summon that unanswering figure to the gay little breakfast-table. Phillida would leave her place behind the burnished copper percolator she prized so highly and come running up the stairs. In her gentleness she would grieve, no doubt. I was sorry for that. But it was a contentment and pleasure for me to recall that I had settled my financial affairs so that my little cousin would never lack money or know any care that I could spare her. Strange, how she had been rated below more beautiful or more clever women until the waif Ethan Vere had set her dearness in full sun for us to wonder at!

"Pygmy, will you think of another pygmy now?" raged the Thing. "Yourself! Think of yourself! Crouch! Think of death, corruption, the vileness of the grave. Think how you are of the grave. Think how you are alone with me. Think how you are abandoned to me."

But with that tenderness for Phillida a warmth had flowed through me like strength.

"Not so," my defiance answered It. "For where I am, I stand by my own will. With where I shall stand, you have nothing to do. Back, then, for with the death of my body your power ends. Back—or else face me, Thing of Darkness, while we stand in one place."

At this mad challenge of mine silence closed down like a shutting trap. Consciousness sank away from me with a sense of swooning quietness.

I stood before the Barrier on the ghostly frontier; erect, arms folded, fronting the Breach in that inconceivably mighty wall. Above, away out of vision on either hand stretched the gray glimmering cliffs.

This I had seen before. But behind me lay that which I had not seen. The mists I believed to be eternal had lifted. Naked, a vast gray sea stretched parallel with the Barrier; like it, without end or even a horizon to bound its enormous desolation. Between these two immensities on the narrow strand at the foot of the wall, I stood, pygmy indeed. In the Breach, as of old, the Thing whose home was there reared Itself against me.

"Man," It spat, "would you see me? Would you see the Eyes once seen by the witch-woman, who fell blasted out of human ken? Creature of clay, crumbling now in the sea of mortality, do you brave my immemorial age?"

It reared up, up, a towering formlessness. It stooped, a lowering menace.

"Man, whenever man has summoned Evil since the youngest days of the world have I not answered? Have I not brought my presence to the magician's lamp? Have I not shadowed the alchemist at his crucible? When the woman called upon me with ancient knowledge, did I not come. I am the guardian of the Barrier. Whoever would pass this way must pass me. Have you the power? Die, then, and begone."

With a long heaving sound of waters in movement, the gray sea stirred from its stillness. As if drawn to some center out of sight, the tide began to recede down that strange beach. Then realization came to me that here was the ocean which, invisible, had surged icy death upon me a while past. The ocean now gathered for the final wave that should overwhelm the defeated.

"Braggart!" my thought answered the taunt. "If the witch-woman was yours, the girl Desire is mine. This I know: as little as man has to do with you, so little have you to do with the human and the good. Living or dead, our path is not yours. I did not summon you. I do dare look upon you, if you have visible form."

Now in the hush a sound that I had faintly heard as a continuing thing seemed to draw nearer. A sound of light, swift footsteps hurrying, hurrying; the steps of one in pitiful eagerness and haste. But I heeded this slightly. My gaze was upon that which took place within the cleft in the great wall. For there the cold darkness was writhing and turning, visible, yet obscure; as the rapids of a glassy, twisting river might look by night. And as one might glimpse beneath the smooth boil and heave of such a river the dim shape of crocodile or water-monster, so in that moving dark there seemed to lie Something from which the mind shrank, appalled. Now gigantic tentacles rolled about a central mass, groping out in unsatisfied greed. Now an ape-like shape seemed to stalk there, rearing up its monstrous stature until all that Breach was choked with it. It fell down into vagueness, where huge coils upraised and sank their loops. But through all change steadily fixed upon me I felt the eyes of the Unseen.

I stood my ground. With what pain and draining cost to my poor endurance there is no need to say. Each instant I anticipated the surge of that returning sea whose flood should smother out the human spark upon its shore. This I had brought upon myself. Yes, and would again to help Desire Michell! If I had sheltered her for one hour — —!

The Thing halted, stooped.

"Man, cast off the woman," It snarled at me. "Fool, evil goes with her. For her you suffer. Thrust her from your breast."

I looked down. Wavering against my breast, just above my heart glimmered a spot of light. The little hurrying steps had ceased. I thought, if the bright head of Desire Michell were rested there against me, how I would strive to shield her from sight of the Thing yonder. In the sweep of that will to protect, I drew my coat about the spot of hovering brightness.

I felt her press warm against me. I heard the roar of the death-wave far out in that sea. Before me— —

Oh Horror of the Frontier, what broke through the dread Breach. What formed there, more inhuman from Its likeness to humanity? What Hand reached for me— for—us— —

CHAPTER XVI

"I have had a dream past the wit of man to say what dream it was."

—Midsummer Night's Dream.

"Mr. Locke! Mr. Locke!"

I opened heavy eyes to meet the eyes of Ethan Vere, who bent over me. Phillida was there, too, pale of face. But what was That just vanishing into the darkness beyond my window-sill? What malignant glare seared disappointment and grim promise across my consciousness? Had I brought with me or did I hear now a whispered: "*Pygmy, again!*"

"Cousin, Cousin, are you very ill?" Phillida was half sobbing. "Won't you drink the brandy, please? Oh, Ethan, how cold he is to touch!"

"Hush, dear," Vere bade, in his slow steadfast way. "Mr. Locke, can you swallow some of this?"

I became aware that his arm supported me upright in my chair while he held a glass to my lips. Mechanically I drank some of the cordial. Vere put down the glass and said a curious thing. He asked me:

"Shall I get you out of this room?"

Why should he ask that, since the spectre was for me alone? Or if he had not seen It, how did he know this room was an unsafe area? My stupefied brain puzzled over these questions while I managed a sign of refusal. Any effort was impossible to me. The cold of the unearthly sea still numbed my body. My heart labored, staggering at each beat.

Vere's support and nearness were welcome to me. His tact let me rest in the mute inaction necessary to recovery, while my body, astonished that it still lived, hesitatingly resumed the task of life. Somehow he reassured and directed Phillida. Presently she was busied with the coffee apparatus in the corner of the room.

It was too much weariness even to turn my eyes aside from the expanse of the table before me. The vase was upset, I noted, as I had seemed to see it. The spray of purple heliotrope Phillida had put there the day before lay among the wet sheets of music. The Book of Hermas lay open at the page I had last turned, the rosy lamplight upon the text.

"*Behold, I saw a great Beast that he might devour a city—whose name is Hegrin. Thou hast escaped—because thou didst not fear for so terrible a Beast. If, therefore, ye shall have prepared yourselves, yet may escape— —"*

What did they mean, the old, old words men have rejected? What had Hermas glimpsed in his visions? How many men are written down liars because they traveled in strange lands indeed, and explorers, strove to report what they had seen? Who before me had stood at the Barrier and set foot on the Frontier between the worlds?

The fog still dense outside was whitening with daybreak. A few hours while the sun ran its course once more for me, then night again, bringing completion of the menace. I recognized that this delay could not affect the end. Perhaps it would have been easier if all had finished for me tonight, easier if Vere and Phillida had not found me in time to bring me back.

How had they found out my condition? Wonder stirred under my lethargy. Had I called or cried out? It did not seem that I could have done so. Certainly I had not tried! I was not quite so poor an adventurer as that.

Phillida was back with a cup of steaming black coffee, tiptoeing in her anxiety and questioning Vere with her eyes. He took the cup, stooping to receive my glance of assent to the new medicine.

The brandy had stimulated, but sickened me. The coffee revived me so much that I was able to take the second cup without Vere's help. When I had walked up and down the room a few times, leaning on his arm, life had taken me back, if only for a little while.

The two nurses were so good in their care of me that our first words were of my gratitude to them. Then my curiosity found voice.

"How did you happen to come in at this hour?" I asked. "How did you know I was—ill?"

"I cannot imagine what made Ethan wake up," said Phillida, with a puzzled look toward her husband. "He woke me by rushing out of the room and letting the door slam behind him. Of course I knew something must be wrong to make Drawls hurry like that. Usually he does such a tremendous lot in a day while looking positively lazy. So I came rushing after and found him in here, trying to waken you. I—I thought at first that you were not living, Cousin Roger. It was horrible! You were all white and cold— —" she shivered.

Vere poured another cup of coffee. He said nothing on the subject, merely observing that the stimulant would hardly hurt me and some might be good for Phil. I asked her to bring cups for them both.

"I am not sure I really care about the coffee, but I'll make some more," she nodded, dimpling. "I love to drink from your wee porcelain cups with their gold holders. You do have pretty things, you bachelors from town."

When she was across the room, I asked quietly:

"What was it, Vere? What sent you to me?"

He answered in as subdued a tone, looking at the tinted shade of the lamp instead of at my face.

"The young lady woke me, Mr. Locke. She came to the bedside, whispering that you were dying—would be dead if I didn't get to help you in time. She was gone before Phillida roused up so she doesn't know anything about it."

My heart, so nearly stopped forever and so lethargic still, leaped in a strong beat. Desire, then, had come back to save me. For all my doubt and seemingly broken faith, she had brought her slight power to help me in my hour of danger. For my sake she had broken through her mysterious seclusion to call Vere and send him to my rescue.

Neither he nor I being unsophisticated, I understood what Vere believed, and why he looked at the lamp rather than at me. But even that matter had to yield precedence to my first eagerness.

"You saw her?" I demanded. "You call her young. You saw her face, then?"

"I could forget it if I had," he said dryly. "As it happened, I didn't. She was wrapped in a lot of floating thin stuff; gray, I guess? The room was pretty dark, and I was jumping out of sleep. I don't know why she seemed young unless it was the easy, light way she moved. By the time I got what she was saying and sat up, she was gone."

"Gone?"

"She went out the door like a puff of smoke. I just saw a gray figure in the doorway, where the hall lamp made it brighter than in the room. When I came into the hall there wasn't a sign of anybody about. Nor afterward, either!"

I considered briefly.

"I suppose I know what you are thinking, Vere. It is natural, but wrong. The lady——"

"Mr. Locke," he checked me, "I'm not—thinking. I guess you're as good a judge as I am about what goes on in this house. After the way you've treated us from the first, I'd be pretty dull not to know you're as choice of Phillida as I am; and she is all that matters."

"Who is?" demanded Phillida, returning. "Me? I haven't the least idea what you are talking about, Drawls, but I think Cousin Roger matters a great deal more than I do, just now. Perhaps now he is able to tell us about this attack, and if he should have a doctor. I have noticed for weeks how thin and grave he has been growing to be. If only he *would* drink buttermilk!"

I looked into the candid, affectionate face she turned to me. From her, I looked to her husband, whose New England steadiness had been tempered by a sailor's service in the war and broadened by the test of his experience in a city cabaret. A new thought cleaved through my perplexities like an arrow shot from a far-off place.

"How much do you both trust me?" I slowly asked. "I do not mean trust my character or my good intentions, but how much confidence have you in my sanity and commonsense? Would you believe a thing because I told it to you? Or would you say: 'This is outside usual experience. He is deceiving us, or mad'?"

They regarded one another, smiling with an exquisite intimacy of understanding.

"Don't you see yourself one little, little bit, Cousin?" she wondered at me.

"Anything you say, goes all the way with us," Vere corroborated.

"Wait," I bade. "Drink your coffee while I think."

"Please drink yours, Cousin Roger, all fresh and hot."

I emptied the cup she urged upon me, then leaned my forehead in my hands and tried to review the situation. They obeyed like well-bred children, settling down on a cushioned seat together and taking their coffee as prettily as a pair of parakeets. They seemed almost children to me, although there was little difference in years between Vere and myself. But then, I stood on the brink where years stopped.

With the next night, my triumphant enemy could be put off no longer. That I could not doubt. I cannot say that I was unafraid, yet fear weighed less upon me than a heavy sense of solemnity and realization of the few hours left during which I could affect the affairs of life. What remained to be done?

On one of my visits to New York, I had called on my lawyer and made my will. There were a few pensioners for whom provision should continue after my death. The aged music master under whom I developed such abilities as I had, who was crippled now by rheumatism and otherwise dependent on a hard-faced son-in-law; the three small daughters of a dead friend, an actor, whose care and education at a famous school of classic dancing I had promised him to finance—a few such obligations had been provided for, and the rest was for Phillida.

But now, what of Desire Michell?

She had seemed so apart from common existence that I never had thought of her possible needs any more than of the needs of a bird that darted in and out of my windows. Until tonight, when I had seen her and she had proved herself all woman by her appeal to Ethan Vere. It was not a spirit or a seeress or "ye foule witch, Desire Michell" who had fled to him for help in rescuing me. It was simply a terrified girl. What was to become of this girl? Under what circumstances did she dwell? Had she a home, or did she need one? Could I care for this matter while I was here?

Day was so far advanced that a clamor of birds came in to us along with a freshening air. The strangely persistent fog had not lifted, but the lamps already looked wan and faded in the new light. I switched them out before speaking to the pair who watched me.

"I have a story to tell you both," I said. "The beginning of it Phillida has already heard. Perhaps——Have you told Vere about the woman who visited this room, the first night I spent in the house? Who cut her hair and left the braid in my hand to escape from me?"

"Yes," she nodded, wide-eyed.

"Will you go to my chiffonier, there in the alcove, and bring a package wrapped in white silk from the top drawer?"

She did as she was asked and laid the square of folded silk before me. I put back the covering, showing that sumptuous braid. The rich fragrance of the gold pomander wrapped with it filled the air like a vivifying elixir. Phillida gathered up the braid with a cry of envious rapture.

"Oh! The gorgeous thing! How do some lucky girls have hair like that? If it was unbound, my two hands could not hold it all. What a pity to have cut it! Look, Ethan, how it crinkles and glitters."

She held it out to him, extended across her palms. Vere refrained from touching the braid, surveying it where it lay. Being a mere bachelor, I had no idea of Phillida's emotions, until Vere's usual gravity broke in a mischievous, heart-warming smile into the brown eyes uplifted to him.

"Beautiful," he agreed politely.

No more. But as I saw the wistful envy pass quite away from my little cousin's plain face and leave her content, I advanced in respect for him.

In the beginning, it was even harder to speak than I had anticipated. When Phillida laid the braid back in its wrapping, I left it uncovered before me and looked at its reassuring reality rather than at my listeners. How, I wondered, could anyone be expected to credit the story I had to tell? How should I find words to embody it?

Only at first! Whether there clung about me some atmosphere of that land between the worlds where I so recently had stood; or the room indeed kept, as I fancied, the melancholy chill of the unseen tide that had washed through it, I met no scepticism from the two who heard my tale of wild experience. They did not interrupt me. Phillida crept close to her husband, putting her hand in his, but she did not exclaim or question.

Silence held us all for a while after I had finished. I had a discouraged sense of inadequacy. After all, they had received but a meagre outline. The color and body of the events escaped speech. How could they feel what I had felt? How could they conceive the charm of Desire Michell, the white magic of her voice in the dark, the force of her personality that could impress her image "sight unseen" beyond all time to erase? How convey to a listener that, understanding her so little, I yet knew her so well?

"I have told you all this because I need your help," I said presently. "Will you give it to me?"

"Go away!" Phillida burst forth. She beat her palms together in her earnestness. "Cousin Roger, take your car and go away—far off! Go where—nothing—can reach you. You must not spend another single night here. Ethan will go with you. I will, too, if you want us. You must not be left alone until you are quite safe; perhaps in New York?"

"And, Desire Michell?"

"She is in no danger, I suppose. She is not my cousin, anyhow. And even she told you to go away."

"You believe my story, then? You do not think me suffering from delusions?"

"Ethan saw the girl, too. If he had not come here in time to save you, I believe you would have died in that terrible stupor. Besides, I have seen for weeks that something was changing you."

"What does Vere say?" I questioned, studying the absorbed gravity of his expression. I wondered what I myself would have said if anyone had brought me such a story.

He passed his arm around Phillida and drew her to him with a quieting, protective movement. His regard met mine with more significance than he chose to voice.

"I'm satisfied to take the thing as you tell it, Mr. Locke," he answered. "Phil is right, it seems to me, about you not staying here. I don't think the young lady ought to stay, either."

"She refuses to leave, Vere. What can I offer her that I have not offered? How can I find her? You have heard how I searched the countryside for a hint of such a girl's presence. No one has ever seen her; or else someone lies very cleverly."

In the pause, Phillida hesitatingly ventured an idea:

"Perhaps she is not—real. If the monster is a ghost thing, may not she be one, too? If we are to believe in such things at all——? She almost seems to intend that you shall believe her the ghost of the witch girl in that old book."

I shook my head with the helpless feeling of trying to explain some abstruse knowledge to a child. I had spoken of the colossal spaces, the solemn immensities of the place where I had set my human foot. I had tried to paint the desolate bleakness of that Borderland where the unnamed Thing and I met, each beyond his own law-decreed boundary, and locked in combat bitter and strong. Phillida had listened; and talked of ghosts the bugbears of grave-yard superstition. Did Vere comprehend me better? Did he visualize the struggle, weirdly akin to legends of knight and dragon, as prize of which waited Desire Michell; forlornly helpless as white Andromeda chained to her black cliff? Could the Maine countryman, the cabaret entertainer, seize the truths glimpsed by Rosicrucians and mystics of lost cults, when the highly bred college girl failed?

It seemed so. At least his dark eyes met mine with intelligence; hers held only bewilderment and fear.

"They are not ghosts," I said only.

"But how can you be sure?" she persisted.

Beneath the braid and the pomander lay the sheet of paper on which Desire had written weeks before; the first page of that composition now pouring gold into my hands. This I passed to Phillida.

"Do ghosts write?" I queried.

She read the lines aloud.

"'We walk upon the shadows of hills, across a level thrown, and pant like climbers.'"

"They do write, people say, with ouija boards and mediums," she murmured.

I looked at Vere with despair of sustaining this argument. He stood up as if my appeal had been spoken, drawing her with him.

"Now that it's a decent hour, don't you think Cristina might give us some breakfast?" he suggested. "I guess bacon and eggs would be sort of restoring. If you feel up to taking my arm as far as the porch, Mr. Locke, the fresh air might be good medicine, too."

I have speculated sometimes upon how civilized man would get through days not spaced by his recurrent meals into three divisions. Those meals are hyphens between his mind and his body, as it were. What sense of humor can view too intensely a creature who must feed himself three times a day? Are we not pleasantly urged out of our heroics and into the normal by breakfast, luncheon and dinner? Deny it as we will, when we do not heed them we are out of touch with nature.

We went downstairs.

After breakfast was over, Vere and I walked across the orchard to a seat placed near the lake. There I sat down, while he remained standing in his favorite attitude: one foot on a low boulder, his arm resting on his knee as he gazed into the shallow, amber-tinted water. Fog still overlay the countryside, but without bringing coolness. The damp heat was stifling, almost tropical as the sun mounted higher in the hidden sky.

I watched my companion, waiting for him to speak. He appeared intent upon the darting movements of a group of tiny fish, but I knew his thoughts were afar.

"Mr. Locke, I didn't want to speak before Phillida, because it would not do any good for her to hear what I have to say," he finally began. "It is properly the answer to what you asked upstairs, about our believing you had not imagined that story. Did anything slip out over the window-sill when you were waking up?"

Startled, for I had not spoken of this, I met his gaze.

"Yes. Did you see— —"

"Nothing, exactly. Something, though! Like—well, like something pouring itself along; a big, thick mass. Something sort of smooth and glistening; like black, oily molasses slipping over. Only alive, somehow; drawing coils of itself out of the dark into the dark. I can't put it very plain."

"What did you think?"

"The air in the room was bad and close, hard to breathe. I guessed maybe I was a little dizzy, jumping out of bed the way I did and finding you like dead, almost." He paused, and returned his contemplation to the fish darting in the lake.

"That is what I thought," he concluded. "What I felt—well, it was the kind of scare I didn't use to know you could feel outside of bad dreams; the kind you wake up from all shaking, with your face and hands dripping sweat. That isn't all, either!"

This time the pause was so long that I thought he did not mean to continue.

"My excuse for speaking of such matters before Phillida is that I may need a woman friend for Desire Michell," I reverted to the implied rebuke I acknowledged his right to give. "I wanted her help, and yours. More than ever, since you have shared my experience so far, I want your advice."

"I'll be proud to give it, in a minute. First, it's only fair to say I've felt enough wrong around here to be able to understand a lot that once I might have laughed at. Nothing compared to you! But—I've been working about the lake sometimes after dark or before daylight was strong, when a kind of horror would come over me—well, I'd feel I had to get away and into the house or go crazy. That morning when you called from your window to ask where I'd been so early, and I told you looking for turtles—that was one time. I had gone out looking for turtles, but that horror drove me in. When you hailed me, I had it so bad that I could just about make out not to run for the house like a scared cat, yelling all the way. Turning back to the lake with you was a poser. But I did; and the feeling was all gone as quick as it came. We had a nice morning's shooting. Once in a while I've felt it sort of driving me indoors when I stepped off the porch or over to the barn at night. That's a funny thing: the fear was always outside, not in the house. I thought of that while you were telling us how the Thing at the window kept trying to get in at you. We haven't got a haunted house, but a haunted place!"

"Why have you not spoken of this before?" I asked, deeply stirred.

He made a gesture, too American to be called a shrug. He said nothing, watching a large bubble rise through the pure, brown-green water, float an instant on the surface, then vanish with the abrupt completeness of a miniature explosion. I watched also, with an always fresh interest in the pretty phenomenon. Then I repeated my question, rather impatiently as I considered what a relief his companionship in experience would have afforded all these weeks.

"Why not, Vere?"

"Mr. Locke, I don't like to keep saying that you never exactly got used to me as your cousin's husband," he reluctantly replied. "But I can see it's a kind of surprise to you right along that I don't break down or break out in some fashion. Of course I haven't known that you were meeting queer times, too! If you hadn't been through any of this, what would you have thought if I'd come to you with stories of the place being haunted by something nobody could see? You would have judged I was a liar, trying to fix up an excuse for getting away from the work here and shoving off. I don't want to go away. I don't intend to go. I can't see any need of it for Phil and me. But—and this is the advice you spoke of! I think you ought to leave and leave now. It's little better than suicide to stay."

"And abandon Desire Michell?"

He turned his dark observant eyes toward me.

"If I said yes, you wouldn't do it. Phil and I will take care of the young lady, if she will let us. Couldn't a note be left for her, telling her to come to us?"

I shook my head.

"She would not come. Now, less than ever— —" I broke off, shot with sharp self-reproach at the memory of how I had driven her from me last night.

"You won't be any help to her if you're dead," he bluntly retorted.

At that I rose and walked a few paces to knock out my post-breakfast pipe against an apple-tree. I was not so sure that he was right, self-evident as his statement appeared. Ideas moved confusedly in my mind, convictions somehow impressed when that golden-bronze spot of light so gently came to rest above my heart when I last stood at the Barrier; the light so like the bright imagined head of Desire. To fly from my place now, herded like a cowardly sheep by the Thing of the Frontier, would that not be to thrust her away to save myself?

No! Not myself, my life!

I had the answer now. I walked back to Vere and took my seat again.

"Both of us, or neither," I told him. "If you can help me make it both by any ingenuity, I shall be mighty glad. It's a pleasant world! But we will not talk any more of my running for New York like a kicked pup. The question is, will you and Phillida take care of the lady who calls herself Desire Michell, if tomorrow morning finds her free, but alone and friendless?"

"As long as we live, Mr. Locke," he answered. "But I guess there isn't any disgrace in your going to New York, running or not, if you take her with you. And that is what ought to have been done long ago."

"Vere?"

He nodded.

"You've got me! Just pick the lady up, carry her out of that room, and have a show-down. Put her in your car and take her to town."

"I gave her my word not— —"

"People can't stand bowing to each other when the ship's afire. If she is worth dying for, she doesn't want you to die for her."

The simplicity of it! And, leaping the breach of faith, the temptation!

What harm could I do Desire by this plan of Vere's? What good might I not do her? Was it mere slavishness of mind on my part not to overrule her timid will? She must pardon me when she realized my desperate case. A dying man might be excused for some roughness of haste, surely. Whether flight could save us I did not know. I did know absolutely that my enemy had crossed the Barrier last night, and I was prey merely withheld from It by the chance respite of a few daylight hours.

Suppose our escape succeeded? A whole troup of pictures flitted across the screen of my fancy. Desire beside me in the city, my wife. Desire in those delightful shops that make Fifth Avenue gay as a garden of tulips, where I might buy for her frocks and hats, shoes of conspicuous frivolity and those long white gloves that seem to caress a woman's arm—everything fair and fine. Restaurants I had described for her, where she might dine in silken ease and perhaps hear played the music she had named — —

I aroused myself and looked at Vere.

"You'll do it?" he translated my expression.

"I will, if she gives me the opportunity."

"Do you judge she will?"

"I hope so. Since she went so far as to show herself to you in order to send help to me when I was in danger, I believe she will come to my room tonight if I wait there — —"

He looked at me silently. The consternation and protest in his face were speech enough.

"If I wait there alone," I finished somewhat hurriedly. "If she comes in time, we will try the plan. Have the car ready. You and Phillida will be prepared, of course. We will waste no time in getting away as far as possible."

"And if that Thing comes before she does, Mr. Locke?"

"Is there any other way?"

"I guess you haven't considered that you're inviting me to stand by while you get yourself killed," he said stiffly. "I'm not an educated man. I never heard the names you mentioned this morning of people who used to study out things like this. I never heard of any worlds except earth and heaven and hell. But then I couldn't explain how an electric car runs. I know the car does run; and I know you nearly died last night. If you go back and stay alone in that room, we both know what you are going to meet."

I turned away from him because I sickened at the prospect he evoked. The memory of that death-tide was too near and rolled too coldly across the future. If the trial had been hard when mercifully unanticipated, what would it be to meet my enemy now that I knew myself conquered? Would It not deliberately forestall Desire's coming, tonight?

"Mightn't you help the lady more if you went away now, and came back?" he urged.

The deserter's argument, time without end! Was I to fall as low as that?

Phillida's voice called to Vere from the veranda, summoning him to some need of farm or household.

"In a moment, Pretty," he called assent.

But he did not move. I guessed that he hoped much from my silence and would not disturb me lest my decision be hindered or changed.

By and by I stood up.

"Vere, in your varied experiences in peace and war, did you ever chance to meet a coward?"

"Once," he answered briefly.

"And, did you like the sight?"

"No."

"Then," I said, "let us not invite one another to that display. Shall we go in to Phillida?"

CHAPTER XVII

"They say—
What say they?
Let thame say!"

—Old Scottish Inscription.

After luncheon, I drove over to the village with Phillida, who had some house-wifely orders to give at the shops. On second thoughts, Vere and I had agreed to tell her nothing about the venture we planned for tonight. We had satisfied her by the assurance that I meant to start for New York before the dangerous hours after midnight. Reassured, she regained her usual spirits with the buoyancy of her few years and healthy nerves. I gathered her secret belief was that no "ghost" would dare face Ethan.

Which may have been quite true!

On our way home, we stopped at the shop of Mrs. Hill to add to our supply of eggs, Phillida's hens having unaccountably failed to supply their quota. I went in, leaving my companion in the car.

No one else was in the shop. An impulse prompted me to put a question to the little woman whose life had been spent in this neighborhood.

"Mrs. Hill, did you ever hear of anyone named Desire Michell?" I asked.

She stopped counting eggs and blinked up at me. Her sallow, wrinkled face lightened with curiosity and an absurd primness.

"Now, Mr. Locke! I'd like to know where a young city feller like you got that old story from?"

"I have not got it. I want you to tell it to me. She was a witch?"

"She was a hussy," said Mrs. Hill severely. "I was a little girl when she ran away from her father's respectable house, fifty-odd years ago. The disgrace killed him, being a clergyman. An' the gossip that came back, later, an' pictures of her in such dresses! Dear! Dear! The wicked certainly have opportunities."

"Fifty years ago!" I echoed, dazed by this intrusion of a third Desire Michell.

"Ah! Nearly seventy she'd be if she was alive today; which she ain't. Why, she changed her name to one fancier that you might have heard talk of? She was——"

The name she gave me I shall not set down. It is enough to say it was that of a super-woman whose beauty, genius and absolute lack of conscience set Europe ablaze for a while. A torch of womanhood, quenched at the highest-burning hour of her career by a sudden and violent death.

"There was an older house once, on your place," she added pensively. "Did you know that? It stood in the hollow where your lake is now. Two—three hundred years old, folks say it was. One night it burned down in a big thunderstorm. The Michells then living had your house built over by the orchard, then, an' had a dam built across so as to cover up the old site with water. All the Michells lived there till the last one went missionary abroad an' died in foreign parts. I mean the hussy's brother. He took up his father's work, feelin' a strong call. He was only a young boy when his sister went off, but he felt it dreadful. He was a hard man on the sinner. Preached hell and damnation all his days, he did. Lean over the pulpit, he would, his eyes flamin' fire an' his tongue shrivellin' folks in their pews, I can tell you!"

"He left children?" I asked.

"No, sir! Rev'rund never married. He felt women a snare. Land, not much snarin' with what farm women get to wear around here! I've kind of thought of one of those blue foulard silks with white spots into it since before I married Hill, but never came any nearer than pricin' it an' bringin' home a sample. He was death on sweet odors an' soft raiment. Only sweet odors I ever get are the ten-cent bottles Hill makes the pedlar throw in when we trade. I do fancy *Jockey Club* for special times, an' I've got a reasonable hope of salvation, too. I notice your cousin, Mrs. Vere, has scent on her handkerchief week days as well as when she's goin' somewhere, so I guess you don't hold with the Rev'rund Michell in New York?"

I laughed with her as I took up the bag of eggs.

"Did the runaway sister leave any children?" I queried.

"Not a Michell alive anywhere," she asserted positively. "Dead, all dead! The Rev'rund was buried at his mission in some outlandish place. An' if those heathen women dress like I've seen in the movin' picture palace in the village, I don't know how he makes out to rest with them flauntin' past his grave!"

I went thoughtfully out to the car. Indeed, I drove home in such abstraction that Phillida reproved me.

"'The cat has stolen your tongue,'" she teased. "Or did Mrs. Hill vamp you and make roast meat of your heart with her eyes?"

"Phil, do you put scent on your handkerchief week days as well as Sundays?" I shook off thought to inquire.

"No; I keep sachet in my handkerchief box. Why?"

"Next time you are in town, will you buy a blue silk foulard dress with white spots in it and the largest bottle of Jockey Club Extract on sale, and give them to Mrs. Hill for a Christmas present? I'll give you a blank check."

"Cousin Roger? Why?"

So I told her why. But I did not tell her the story of the second Desire Michell; nor of the original house that stood in the hollow now filled by our lake.

Why had a peculiar horror crept through me when Mrs. Hill told me what ruins that water covered? Why had I remembered the inexplicable, repugnant sound that on several occasions had preceded the coming of the Monster; a sound like the smack of huge lips, or some body withdrawn from thick slime? Was entrance into human air open to the alien Thing only through the ruins of the house where It had first been called by the sorceress of long ago?

We were walking across from the garage, after putting away the car, when a recollection flashed upon me. The Metropolitan Museum, in New York, held a portrait by a famous French artist of that incendiary beauty whose name it now appeared cloaked the identity of Desire Michell, daughter and sister of New England clergymen. I had seen the portrait. And piled in an intricate magnificence of curls, puffs and coils about the haughty little head of the lady, was her gold-bronze hair; the color of the braid upstairs in my chiffonier drawer.

I went up to my room and opened the work of Master Abimelech Fetherstone. Yes, there was likeness between the poor, coarse woodcut and the French portrait. The long, dark eyes with their expression of blended drowsiness and watchfulness were too individual to have escaped either record. Moreover, both pictures resembled that face of ivory and dusk I had glimpsed in the ray of the electric torch, all clouded and surrounded by swirls of gray vapor shot with gold.

Who and what was the girl Desire Michell whom I had come to love through a more profound darkness than that of the sight?

It seemed wisest to keep busy for the rest of the afternoon. I sorted my music. There was the score of a musical comedy so nearly completed that it could be sent to those who waited for it. Vere would attend to that, if tonight made it necessary. I reflected with disappointment that the first rehearsals would begin in a couple of weeks, and I had looked forward to this production with especial interest. There was the symphony, still unfinished, that I had hoped might be more enduring than popular music. If I was to be less enduring than either, we must go glimmering on our ways. If I snatched Desire out of her path into mine, she and I would see all those things together.

I finished at last, and set my room in order. There was a fire laid ready for lighting in my hearth, a mere artistic flourish in such weather. I kindled it, and put in the flames three of the volumes from the ancient bookcase. The others were oddities in occult science. Those three were vile and poisonous. No doubt other copies exist, but at least I refused to be guilty of leaving these to wreak their mischief in Phillida's household. They burned quietly enough, and meekly fell to ashes under my poker.

Our round dinner-table was cheerful as usual, with yellow-shaded candles flanking a bowl of yellow and scarlet nasturtiums. But I found its mistress suffering from a nervous headache.

"It is only the fog," she answered our sympathy. "It came on with the evening, somehow. Never mind me. Cristina has made a cream-of-lettuce bisque, and she will never forgive us if we do not eat every bit. Yes, Ethan; of course I'll take mine. I only wish every bush and tree would not drip, drip like a horrid kind of clock ticking; and the foghorns over at the lighthouses *moo* regularly every half minute. And I never heard the waterfall over the dam so loud!"

"We've had a wet summer," Vere observed, soothingly tranquil as ever. "The lake and creek are full. There is more water going over to make a noise."

"Please do not be so frightfully sensible, Drawls. You know I mean a different loudness. It sort of rises up and swims all over one, then dies away."

"Even a fountain will seem to do that if a wind shifts the spray," I suggested.

"Yes, Cousin Roger. But there is no wind tonight."

A discomfort stirred me at the simple reminder. I fancied Vere was similarly affected. If something moved under the water— —?

We changed the conversation to a pergola planned for building next spring, that was to be overrun by grapevines and honeysuckle.

"The grapes shall hang through like an Italian picture," Phillida anticipated, headache forgotten in her enthusiasm. She shook her hair about her pink cheeks, leaning over to outline a pergola with four spoons. "Here in the middle we must have a birdbath. Or no! The birds might peck the grapes. We could have one of those big silver-colored looking-balls on a pedestal to reflect wee views of the garden and lake and sky, with people moving no bigger than dolls. Imagine a reflection of Ethan like a Lilliputian *so* high!"

So I was able to leave her eagerly hunting catalogues of garden ornaments in her sewing-room, when the time came for me to keep my rendezvous with Death or the lady. In spite of my warning gesture, Vere followed me into the hall. His dark face was distressed and anxious.

"Let me go with you," he urged.

"No, thanks. Stay with Phil, and keep her too busy to suspect where I am."

"If I'm doing wrong to let you go," he began.

"You cannot stop me. It is still too early for danger, I think. If you like, you can stroll out on the lawn from time to time and look up at my windows. As long as the lamps are lighted in the room, I am all right. Nothing is happening."

"Your lamps were all three lighted when I found you last night," he said.

The darkness had been only for my eyes, then? Certainly I had seemed to see light withdrawn from the lamps. I mastered a tremor of the nerves, and covered it by stroking Bagheera, who sat on a hall chair making an after-dinner toilet with tongue and paw.

"Well, take care of Phil," I repeated, evading argument.

He detained me.

"The young lady might not come if there were two people, Mr. Locke. I can see that! But I'll go instead. I guess I'd be safer than you, with the—the— —You know what I mean! It would be the first time for me. And if I sat waiting in the dark, the lady couldn't tell you were not there. Of course I'd bring her right to you."

No one could appreciate the courage of that offer so well as we who had both felt the intolerable horror of the nearness of the Thing whose nature was beyond our nature to endure.

"She would come to no one except me," I refused. "But, thank you. And Vere, if what you have said about my feeling toward Phillida's husband was true once, it is true no longer."

His clasp was still warm on my hand when I went into my room and switched on the lights. Soft and colorful, the haunted room sprang into view. The writing-table and piano gleamed bare without their usual burdens of scattered papers and music, removed that afternoon. For lack of familiar occupation, when I sat down in my favorite place, I took up the gold pomander and fell to studying the intricate designs worked in the metal.

"Containing a rare herb of Jerusalem called Lady's Rose, resembling spikenard, with vervain, and cedar, and secret simples — —"

"Vervain, which is powerful against evil spirits — —"

The strange fragrance, heady as the bouquet of rich wine, never cloying, exquisite, might well have seemed magical to the dry Puritans, I mused. It should stay by me tonight, like a promise of her coming.

After I had sat there a while, I turned out the lights.

CHAPTER XVIII

"An excellent way to get a fayrie—and when you have her, bind her!"

—ANCIENT ALCHEMIST'S RECIPE.

In the darkness Time crept along like a crippled thing, slow-moving, hideous. Outside fell the monotonous drip, drip from trees and bushes, likened by Phillida to a horrid clock. The fog was a sounding-board for furtive noises that grew up like fungi in the moist atmosphere. The thought of Phillida and Vere down in the pleasant living room tempted me almost beyond resistance. I wanted to spring up, to rush out of the room; to fling myself into my car and drive full speed until strength failed and gasoline gave out.

Was that the lake which stirred in the windless night? The lake, under which lay the fire-blackened ruins of the house where the first Desire Michell flung open an awful door that her vengeance might stride through!

Was it too late for my Desire to come, and time for the coming of that Other?

The step of Vere sounded on the gravel path where he walked beneath the window. He was making a trip of inspection, and would find no light shining from the room. I was about to rise and call down a word of reassurance to him, when a current of spiced air passed by me. I sat arrested in hope and expectancy.

"Here, after my warning, after last night?" her soft voice panted across the dark. "Will you die, then? Cruel to me, and wicked to come here again! Oh, must I wish you were a coward!"

Every vestige of her calmness gone, she was sobbing as she spoke. I could imagine she was wringing the little hands that once had left a betraying print upon my table's surface.

"I was cruel to you last night, Desire; yet afterward you saved my life by sending Ethan Vere to wake me. Would you have had me leave without meeting you again, neither thanking you nor asking your forgiveness?"

I thought she came nearer.

"For so little, you would brave the Dread One in Its time of triumph? O steadfast soldier, who faces the Breach even in the hour of death, in all that you have done you have remembered me. Why speak of anger or forgiveness? Have I not injured you?"

"Never. I love you."

"Is not that an injury? Even though I hid my ill-omened face from you, reared as I was to sad knowledge of the wrath upon me, the wrong has been done. Weak as water in the test, I kept the letter of my promise and broke the intent. Yet go; keep life at least."

"Desire, I do not understand you," I answered. "No matter for that, now! I am content to share whatever you bring. Not roughly or in challenge as I asked you last night, but earnestly and with humility I ask you to come away with me now. If trouble comes to my wife and me, I do not doubt we can bear it. Let us not be frightened from the attempt. Come."

"I, to take happiness like that?" she marveled in desolate amazement. "No. At least I will go to my own place, if tardily. Roger, be kind to me. Give me a last gift. Let me know that somewhere you are living. Out of my sight, out of my knowledge, but living in the same world with me. Each moment you stay here is a risk."

In that warning she had reason. I rose. It was time to act, but action must be certain. If my groping movements missed her in the dark there might be no second chance.

"Desire, if all is as you say and we are not to meet again as we have done, you shall let me touch you before I go," I said firmly.

"No!"

"Yes. Why, would you have me live all the years to come in doubt whether you were a woman or a dream? Perhaps you might seem at last a phantom of my own sick brain to which faithfulness would be folly? Here across the table I stretch my arm. Lay your palm in my palm. I may die tonight."

Whether she wished it also, or whether my resolve drew obedience, I do not know. But a vague figure moved through the dark toward me. A hand settled in mine with the brushing touch of an alighting bird. I closed my hand hotly upon that one. I sprang a step aside from the table between us, found her, and drew her to me.

What did I hold in my arms? Softness, fragrance, draperies beneath which beat life and warmth. As I stooped to reassure her, her breath curled against my cheek. So with that guide I turned my head, and set my lips on the lips I had never seen.

Did Something uprear Itself out there in the black fog? A cold air rushed across the summer heat of the fog; air foul as if issued from the opened door of a vault. As once before, a tremor quivered through the house. The hanging chains of the lamps swung with a faint tinkling sound.

I snatched Desire Michell off her feet and sprang for the door. Somehow I found and opened it at the first essay. We were out into the hall. With one hand I dragged the door shut behind us, then carried her on to the head of the stairs. There I set her down, but stood before her as a bar against any attempt at escape.

A lamp shed a subdued light above us. I looked at my captive. Never again after that kiss could she deny her womanhood or pose as a phantom. So far my victory was complete. The lady might be angry, but it must be woman's anger. I knew she had not suspected my intention until I lifted her in my arms. She had struggled then, after her defenses had fallen.

She was quiet now, as though the light had quelled her resistance. She stood drooped and trembling; not the old-time witch, not the dazzling adventuress, only a small fragile girl wound and wrapped in some gray stuff that even covered the brightness of her hair. Her face was held down and showed no more color than a water-lily.

"I thought," she whispered, just audibly. "I thought you—would say, good-bye!"

"I know," I stammered. "But I could not. That way was impossible for us."

She did not contradict me. She was so very small, I saw, that her head would reach no higher than where the bright spot had rested above my heart when I had last stood at the Barrier. One hand gripped the veils beneath her chin, and seemed the clenched fist of a child.

The crash of my door had startled the household. I had heard Phillida cry out, and Vere's running steps upon the gravel path. Now he came springing up the stairs. At the head of the flight he stopped, staring at us.

"Desire," I spoke as naturally as I could manage, "this is Mr. Vere. Vere, my fiancée, Miss Michell. Shall we go down to Phillida?"

And Desire Michell did not deny my claim.

I am not very sure of how we found ourselves downstairs. Nor do I remember in what words we made the two girls known to one another. Presently we were all in the living room, and Phillida had possession of Desire Michell while Vere and I looked on stupidly at the proceedings.

Phil had placed her in a chair beside a tall floor-lamp and gently drew off the draperies that hooded her. With little murmurs of compassion, she unbound and shook free her guest's hair.

"My dear, you are all damp! This awful fog! You must have been out a long time? You shall drink some tea before we start. Drawls, will you light the alcohol lamp on the tea-table? The kettle is filled."

Now I could understand how Desire had appeared amid a drift of fireshot smoke in the beam of my electric torch, the night before. Her hair was a garment of flame-bright silk flowing around her, curling and eddying in rich abundance. Over this she had worn the gray veils to smother all that color and sheen into neutral sameness with night and shadows. No wonder her face had seemed wraith-like when her startled shrinking away from the light had set all that drapery billowing about her.

She was the voice that had been my intimate comrade through weeks of strange adventure. She was the woman of the faded, yellow book, and the painted beauty at the Metropolitan. She was all the Desires of whom I had ever dreamed; and she was none of them, for she was herself. Her long dark eyes, suddenly lifted to me, were individual by that ancestral blending of drowsiness with watchfulness; yet were akin to the eyes of youth in all times by their innocence. Her mouth, too, was the soft mouth of a young girl kept apart from sordid life. But her forehead, the noble breadth between the black tracery of her eyebrows, expressed the student whose weird, lofty knowledge had so often abashed my ignorance.

Only my ignorance? Now as she looked at me across the room, all self-confidence trickled away from me. What distinguished me from a thousand men she might meet on any city street? What had I ever said worth note in the hours we had spent together? Now she saw me in the light, plainly commonplace; and remembering myself lame, I stood amazed at the audacity with which I had laid claim to her.

She was rising from the chair, gently putting aside Phillida's detaining hands. She had not spoken one word since her faltered speech to me, upstairs. Neither Vere nor Phillida had heard her voice. She had given her hand to each of them and submitted to Phil's care with a docility I failed to recognize in my companion of the dark. Her decisive movement now was more like the Desire Michell I knew. Only, what was she about to do? Repudiate my violence and me—perhaps go back to her hiding-place?

She came straight to where I stood, not daring even to advance toward her. We might have been alone in the room. I rather think we were, to her preoccupation.

"You must go away," she said. "If there is any hope, it is in that. Nothing else matters, now; nothing! If you wish, take me with you. It would be wiser to leave me. But nothing really matters except that you should not stay here. I will obey you in everything if you will only go. Take your car and drive—drive fast—anywhere!"

It is impossible to convey the desperate urgency and fervor of her low voice. Phillida uttered an exclamation of fear. Vere wheeled about and left the room. The front door closed behind him. The gravel crunched under his tread on the path to the garage, and the rate at which the light he carried moved through the fog showed that he was running. He obviously accepted the warning exactly as it was given. After the briefest indecision, Phillida hurried out into the hall.

For my part, I did nothing worth recording. I had made discovery of two places where I was not the "lame feller." And if the first place was the dreary Frontier, the second country was that rich Land of Promise in Desire Michell's eyes.

What we said in our brief moment of solitude is not part of this account.

Phillida was back promptly, her arms full of garments. With little murmurs of explanation by way of accompaniment, she proceeded to invest Desire in a motor coat and a dark-blue velvet hat rather like an artist's tam-o'shanter. I noticed then that the girl wore a plain frock of gray stuff, long of sleeve and skirt, fastened at the base of her throat with severe intent to cover from sight all loveliness of tint and contour. Nothing farther from the fashion of the day or the figure of my cousin could be imagined.

"You must wear the coat because it is always cool motoring at night," Phillida was murmuring. "And of course you will want it at a hotel; until you can do some shopping. I will just tie back your gorgeous, scrumptious hair with this ribbon, now. I know I haven't enough hairpins to put it up without wasting an awful lot of time, but we will buy them in the morning. We are going to take the very best care of you every minute, so you must not worry."

"You are so kind to me," Desire began tremulously. "No one was ever so kind! It does not matter about me, or what people think of me, if he will only go from here quickly."

"Right away," Phillida soothed. "My husband has gone for the car. I hear him coming now!"

In fact, Vere was coming up the veranda steps. His hand was on the knob of the outer door, fumbling with it in a manner not usual to him, then the knob yielded and he was inside.

"But how slow you are, Drawls," his wife called, with an accent of wonder.

Vere crossed the threshold of the room, his gaze seeking mine. He was pale, and drops of fog moisture pearled his dark face like sweat.

"I am sorry, Mr. Locke," he addressed me, ignoring the others. "Perhaps you felt that shake-up, a quarter-hour ago? Like a kind of earthquake, or the kick from a big explosion a long ways off? It didn't seem very strong to me. It was too strong for that old tree by the garage, though! Must have been decayed clear through inside. Willows are like that, tricky when they get old."

"Ethan, what *are* you talking about?" cried Phillida, aghast.

He continued to look at me.

"I guess it must have fallen just about when you slammed your door upstairs. Seems I do remember a sort of second crash following the noise you made. I was too keen on finding out what was happening up there to pay much heed."

"Well, Vere?"

"Tree smashed down through the roof of the garage," he reluctantly gave his report. "Everything under the hood of the automobile is wrecked. There is no motor left, and no radiator. Just junk, mixed up with broken wood and leaves and pieces of the stucco and tiles of the garage."

So there was to be no going tonight from the house beside the lake. A frustrated group, we stood amid our preparations; the two girls wearing cloaks and hats for the drive that would never be taken. Had we ever really expected to go? Already the project was fading into the realm of fantastic ideas, futile as the pretended journeys of children who are kept in their nursery. Desire lifted her hands and took off the blue velvet cap with a resignation more expressive than words. Only my practical little cousin charged valiantly at all obstacles.

"We aren't ever going to give up?" she cried protest. "Cousin Roger? Ethan? *You* cannot mean to give up. Why—'phone to the nearest garage to send us another car. If we pay them enough they will drive anywhere. Or if they cannot take us to New York, they will take us to the railroad station where we can get a train for some place. Can't we, Drawls?"

"We could," Vere admitted. "I'd admire to try it, anyhow. But the telephone wire came across the place right past the garage, you know— —"

"The tree tore the wire down, too?"

"I'm afraid it snapped right in two, Phil."

"We—we might walk," she essayed.

But even her brave voice trailed into silence as she glanced toward the black, dripping night beyond the windows.

"Or if we found a horse and wagon," she murmured a final suggestion.

Vere shook his head.

"Come!" I assumed charge with a cheerfulness not quite sincere. "None of us are ready for such desperate efforts to leave our cozy quarters here. Especially as I fancy Vere's 'earthquake' was the tremor of an approaching thunderstorm. I felt it, myself. Let us light all the lamps and draw the curtains to shut out the fog which has got on everyone's nerves by its long continuance. We are overwrought beyond reason. Suppose we sit here together, strong in numbers, for the few hours until daylight? I think that should be safeguard enough. Tomorrow we will do all we had planned for tonight. Come in, Vere, and close the door."

He obeyed me at once. Desire Michell passively suffered me to unfasten and take off the coat she wore, too heavy for such a night. She had uttered no word since Vere announced the destruction of the car. She did not speak now, when I put her in the low chair beneath the lamp. I had a greed of light for her, as a protection and because darkness had held her so long.

"It seems as if we should do something!" Phillida yielded unwillingly.

Vere's eyes met mine as he turned from drawing the last curtain. We were both thinking of the force that had driven the frail old willow tree through tile and cement of the new building to flatten the metal of motor and car into uselessness. The mere weight of the tree would not have carried it through the roof. To "do something" by way of physical escape from that— —

The ribbon had glided from Desire's hair, almost as if the vital, resilient mass resentfully freed itself from restraint by the bit of satin. Now she put up her hands with a slow movement and drew two broad strands of the glittering tresses across her shoulders, veiling her face.

"Wait," she answered Phillida, most unexpectedly. "I must be sure—quite sure! I must think. If you will—wait."

CHAPTER XIX

"Oh, little booke—how darst thou put thyself in press for drede?"

—CHAUCER.

We sat quietly waiting. I had drawn a chair near Desire. Phillida and Vere were together, chairs touching, her right hand curled into his left. Bagheera the cat had slipped into the room before the door was closed, and lay pressed against his mistress's stout little boot. Our small garrison was assembled, surely for as strange a defense as ever sober moderns undertook. For my part, it was wonder enough to study that captive who was at once so strange yet so intimately well known to me.

The Tiffany clock on the mantel shelf chimed midnight. Soon after, we began to experience the first break in the heavy monotony of heat and fog that had overlaid the place for three days. The temperature began to fall. The fog did not lift. The flowered cretonne curtains hung straight from their rods unstirred by any movement of air. But the atmosphere in the room steadily grew colder. I saw Phillida shiver in the chill dampness and pull closer the collar of her thin blouse. When Desire finally spoke, we three started as if her low tones had been the clang of a hammer.

"I have tried to judge what is best," she said, not raising her face from its shadowing veil of hair. "I am not very wise. But it seems better that there should be no ignorance between us. If I had been either wise or good, I should never have come down from the convent to draw another into danger and horror without purpose or hope of any good ending."

"The convent?" I echoed, memory turning to the bleak building far up the hillside. "You came from there?"

"There is a path through the woods. I am very strong and vigorous. But I had to wait until all there were asleep before I could come. Sometimes I could not come at all. For this house, I had my father's old key. It was only for this little time while I am being taught. Soon I will put on a nun's dress and cut my hair, and—and never—never leave there any more."

Stupefied, I thought of the black loneliness of the wooded hillside behind us. No wonder the fog was wet upon her hair! Her slight feet had traversed that path night after night, had brought her to the door her key fitted, had come through the dark house to the door of the room upstairs. When she left me, she had toiled that desolate way back. For what? Humility bent me, and bewilderment.

"But why?" Phillida gasped. "Why? Cousin Roger hunted everywhere to find you. He would have gone anywhere you told him to see you. Didn't you know that?"

"I never meant him to see me."

"Why not?"

"I am Desire Michell, fourth of that name; all women who brought misfortune upon those who cared for them," she answered, her voice lower still. "How shall I make you understand? I was brought up to know the wrath and doom upon me, yet I myself can scarcely understand. My father knew all, yet he fell in weakness."

"Your father?" I questioned, recalling Mrs. Hill's positive genealogy of the Michells in which there was no place for this daughter of the line.

"He was the last of his family. When he was very young the conviction came to him that his duty was never to marry, so our race might cease to exist. He lived here and preached against evil. He studied the ancient learning that he might be fitted to wrestle with sin. But in the end horror of what was here gained upon him so that he closed the house and went abroad to work as a missionary. There was a girl; the daughter of the clergyman who was leaving the mission. My father—fell in love. He forgot all his convictions and married her. He knew it was a sin, but it was stronger than he was. She only lived one year. When I was born, she died. He prayed that I would die, too. But—I— —"

Her voice died into silence. I ventured to lean nearer and take her hand into mine.

"Desire," I said, "why should you be a sufferer for the actions of a woman who died over two centuries ago? What is the long dead Desire Michell to you?"

A strange and solemn hush followed my question. The words seemed to take a significance and importance beyond their simple meaning. The hand I held trembled in my clasp. She answered at last, just audibly:

"You know. You said that you had read her book."

"But the book tells so little, Desire. Just such a chronicle of superstition as may be found in a hundred old records."

She shook her head slightly.

"Not that! Bring me the book."

The book was upstairs in the room from which I had carried her half an hour before in something very like a panic flight. Before I could release her hand and rise, before I comprehended his intention, Vere was out of the living room and upon the stairs. It was too late to overtake him. The man who had been a professional skater covered the stairs in a few easy, swinging strides. We heard his light tread on the floor overhead, heard him stop beside the table where the book lay. Then, he was returning. My door closed. His step sounded on the stairs again; in a moment he was back among us, and quietly offering the volume to our guest. His dark eyes met mine reassuringly, deprecating the thoughts I am sure my face expressed.

"Lights burning and all serene up there," he announced.

Desire touched the book with a curious repugnance.

"I was looking for this, the first night I came here," she murmured. "That is why I came to America after my father died. I had promised him to destroy this record. When I heard that the house was sold to a gentleman from New York, I came down from the convent on the hill to find the bookcase holding the old history. I did not know anyone was here, that night, until you touched my hair."

I remembered the bookcase near the bed, where I stood my candle and matches. Unaware, I had prevented her finding the thing she sought, and so forced her to return. Afterward, the house had been full of workmen making alterations and improvements, until later still Phillida had transferred the bookcase and its contents to her sewing room. If I had not taken the whim to sleep in the old house on the night of my purchase, or if I had chosen another room, the existence of Desire Michell might never have been known to me.

Would the creature from the Barrier have appeared to me, if I had not known her?

She was drawing something from behind the portrait of the first Desire Michell; a thin, small book that had lain concealed between the cover of the larger volume and the page bearing the woodcut, where a sort of pocket was formed that had escaped our notice. Laid upon the table, the little book rolled away from the girl's fingers and lay curled upon itself in the lamplight. The limp morocco cover was spotted with mildew and half-revealed pages of close, fine writing blotched in places with rusty stains. It gave out an odor of mould and age in an atmosphere made sweet by Desire's presence.

Phillida, who had been silent even when Vere left her to go upstairs, shrank away from the book on the table. She darted a glance over her shoulder at the curtained windows behind her.

"Drawls, I cannot help what everybody thinks of me," she said plaintively. "I am cold. The fire is ready laid in the grate. Will you put a match to it, please?"

No one smiled at the request. Her husband uttered some soothing phrase of compliance. We all looked on while the flame caught and began to creep up among the apple-logs. Bagheera rose and changed his position to one before the hearth. When Vere stood erect, Desire leaned toward him.

"Will you read, aloud, sir?" she asked of him, and made a gesture toward the morocco book.

She surprised us all by that choice. I was unreasoning enough to feel slighted, although the task was one for which I felt a strong dislike. I fancied Vere liked the idea no better, from his expression. However, he offered no demur, but sat down at the table and began to flatten the warped pages that perversely sprang back and clung about his fingers. Desire slowly turned her lovely eyes to me, eyes that looked by gift of nature as if their long corners had been brushed with kohl. She said nothing, yet somehow conveyed her meaning and intent. I understood that she did not wish to hear me read those pages; that it was painful to her that they should be read at all.

Vere was ready. He glanced around our circle, then began with the simple directness that gave him a dignity peculiarly his own.

"'Mistress Desire Michell, her booke, Beginning at the nineteenth year of her Age,'" he read, in his leisurely voice.

The living Desire Michell and I were regarding one another. I smiled at the quaint wording, but she shuddered, and put her hands across her eyes.

Yet there was nothing in those first pages except a girl's chronicle of village life. This book evidently carried on a diary kept from early childhood; a diary written out of loneliness. Apparently the bare colonial life pressed heavily upon the writer; who, having no companions of the intellect, turned to this record of her own mind as a prisoner might talk to his reflection in a mirror rather than go mad from sheer silence. Discontent and restlessness beat through the lines like fluttering wings. She wrote of her own beauty with a cool appraisal oddly removed from vanity, almost with resentment of a possession she could not use.

"Like a man who finds treasure in a desert isle, I am rich in coin that I may not spend," she wrote. "I stand before my mirror and take a tress of my hair in either hand; I spread wide my arms full reach, yet I cannot touch the end of those tresses. Nor can my two hands clasp the bulk of them. There have been other women who had such hair, who were of body straight and white, and had the eyes—but I cannot read that they stayed poor and obscure."

There followed some quotations from the classics of which I was able to give but vague translations when Vere passed the book to me, both because my knowledge was scanty and because of their daring unconventionality. There were allusions, too, to ladies of later history who had found fairness a broad staircase for ambition to mount. Of the writer's learning, there could be no question; a learning amazing in one so young and so situated. The source of this became apparent. Her father was consumed with the passion of scholarship, and the girl's hungry mind fed in the pastures where he led the way.

Here crept into view an anomaly of character. The austere Puritan divine, whose life was open and blank, bare and cold as a winter field, cherished a secret dissipation of the mind. He labored upon a book on the errors of magic. So laboring, he became snared by the thing he denounced. He believed in the hidden lore while he condemned it. Deeper and deeper into forbidden knowledge his eagerness for research led him. Unsanctioned by any church were the books Dr. Michell starved his body to buy from Jews or other furtive dealers in unusual wares. The titles in his library comprehended the names of more charlatans than bishops. He could define the distinctions between necromancy, sorcery, and magic. The marvelous calculations of the Pythagoreans engaged him, and the lost mysteries of the Cabiri.

From such studies he would arise on the Sabbath to preach sermons that held his dull flock agape. Bitter draughts of salvation he poured for their spiritual drinking. He scarcely saw how any man might escape hell-fire, all being so vile. Against witchcraft and tampering with Satan's agents he was eloquent. He rode sixty miles in midwinter to see a Quaker whipped and a woman hung who had been convicted as a witch.

Of all this, his daughter wrote with an elfin mockery. Her brilliant eye of youth saw through the inconsistency of the beliefs he strove to reconcile. She learned his lore, read his books, and discarded his doctrine.

"I study with him, but I think alone," she set down her independence.

Without his knowledge, she proceeded to actual experiment with rude crucible and alembic in her own chamber. She essayed some age-old recipes of blended herbs and ingredients within her reach, handled at certain hours of the night and phases of the moon. All were innocent enough, it seemed. She cured a beloved old dog of rheumatism and partial blindness. She discovered an exquisite perfume which she named Rose of Jerusalem.

But the experiments were not fortunate, she made obscure complaint. The dog, cured, lived only a few weeks. The perfume, in which she revelled with a fierce, long-denied appetite, steeping her rich hair in it and her severely dull garments, awoke many whispers in a community where sweet odors were unknown and disapproved. She alluded, with a mingling of freezing scorn and triumph, to the young men who followed after her—"seeking a wife who would be at their hearth as fatal a guest as that fair woman sent by an enemy to Alexander the Great, whose honey breath was deadly poison to who so kissed there."

Into this situation rode the fine gentleman from the colonial world of fashion who was to fix the fate of Desire Michell and his own.

From this point on, the diary was a record of the same story as the "History of Ye foule Witch, Desire Michell."

The love affair that followed Sir Austin's visit to the clergyman's house leaped hot and instant as flame from oil and fire brought together. The girl was parched with thirst for life, yet despised all around her. The man was dazzled by a beauty and mentality foreign as a bird of paradise found nested in Connecticut snow. A mad, wild passion linked them that was more than half a duel. For Sir Austin was already betrothed. Honor might not have chained him for long, but his need of his betrothed's fortune proved more enduring. He was a man bred to wealth, who did not possess it. He offered Desire Michell his left hand.

He was turned out of her father's house with a red weal struck across his face like a brand.

Of course he returned. The arrow was firmly fixed. He asked her to marry him, and was refused with savage contempt. He would not take the refusal. Her heart and ambition were hidden traitors to his cause. In the end she surrendered and the marriage day was set.

Sir Austin rode away to set his house in order, while Desire turned from alchemy to make her wedding garments.

The entries during this interval were sweetly gentle and feminine. Her Rose of Jerusalem fragrance was all her own, and was kept so, but she made less-rare essences and sold them through a pedlar in order to buy fine linen and brocade for a trousseau not designed to be worn in a Puritan village. She was happy and at rest in expectation.

On her wedding day the destroying news fell. Sir Austin hid a weak spirit within a strong and handsome body. Away from Desire's glamour, back in New York, he had not broken his engagement to the heiress. Instead, he had married her on the day arranged before he met the clergyman's daughter.

There was never again a connected record in the diary. Pages were torn out in places, entries were broken off, half-made. But the story Vere's slow, steady voice conveyed to us was the one we knew; the one my Desire had told to me the first night I slept in this house. The half-mad girl turned to her father's deadly books. Sir Austin died as his waxen image dissolved before the fire, where the girl sat watching with merciless hate. He died, raving and frothing, on her door-sill. She never saw him after the day he rode away to prepare for their marriage. She set open her window that she might hear his progress to that hard death, but never deigned to turn her glance upon him.

The clergyman was dead, now; of shame, or perhaps of terror at the child he had reared. The girl was alone.

The diary grew wilder, with gaps of weeks where there were no entries. More frequently, pages were missing and paragraphs obliterated by the reddish blotches like rust or blood. There were accounts of weird, half-told experiments ranging through the three degrees of magic set forth by Talmud and Cabala. She wrote of legions of kingdoms between earth and heaven, and the twelve unearthly worlds of Plato. She alluded to a Barrier between men and other orders of beings, beyond which dwelt Those whom the magicians of old glimpsed after long toil and incantation.

"Those of whom Vertabied, the Armenian, says: '*Their orders differ from one another in situation and degree of glory, just as there are different ranks among men, though they are all of one nature.*' They cannot cross nor overthrow this Wall, nor can man alone; but if they and man join together— —One there beyond whispers to me of power, splendor, victory— —"

Days later, there was entered a passage of mad triumph and terror. The Barrier was broken through. Out of the breach issued the One whom she had invited to her silver lamps; colossal, formless, whose approach froze blood and spirit. Eyes of unspeakable meaning glared across the dark, whispers unbearable to humanity beat upon her intelligence and named her comrade.

Now as Vere read this, I felt again that quiver of the house or air he had likened to an earth shock and held responsible for the fall of the willow tree that had destroyed our hope of escape by automobile. I looked at my companions and saw no evidence of anyone having noticed what I had seemed to feel. Vere indeed was pale; while Phillida, who sat beside him, was highly flushed with excitement and wonder as she listened. Desire had not stirred in her chair, except to bend her head so her face was shaded by the loosened richness of her hair. Seeing them so undisturbed, I kept silence. A storm might be approaching, but I made no pretense to myself of believing that shock either thunder or earthquake.

The tone of the diary altered rapidly. At first, the unknown from beyond the wall appalled the woman only by its unhuman strangeness, the repugnance of flesh and blood for its loathly neighborhood. Fear emanated from its presence, seen yet unseen, a blackness moving in the black of night when it visited her. Yet she had courage to endure those awful colloquies. She listened. She strove by the spell and incantation to subdue This to her service, as the demon Orthone served the Lord of Corasse, as Paracelsus was served by his Familiar, or Gyges by the spirit of his ring.

Alas for the sorceress, misguided by legend and fantasy! She had evoked no phantom, but a fact actual as nature always is even if nature is not humanly understood. The Thing was real.

The awe of the magician became the stricken panic of the woman. She had unloosed what she could not bind. She had called a servant, and gained a master. Gone forever were the dreams of power and splendor and triumph. Now she learned that only pure magic can discharge the spirits it has summoned, nor could a murderess attain that lofty art.

We were given a glimpse of a frantic girl crouched in the useless pentagram traced on the floor for her protection, covering her beauty with the cloak of her hair against the eyes that burned upon her between the overturned silver lamps.

A deepening horror gathered about the house of Mistress Desire Michell. The old dame who had been the girl's nurse and caretaker fled the place and fell into mumbling dotage in a night. No child would come near the garden, though fruit and nuts rotted away where they dropped from overripeness. No neighbor crossed the doorstep where Sir Austin had died. She lived in utter solitude by day. By night she waged hideous battle against her Visitor; using woman's cunning, essaying every expedient and art her books suggested to her desperate need.

With each conflict, her strength and resource waned, while That which she held at bay knew no weariness. Time was not, for it, nor change of purpose.

"I faint, I fail!" she wrote. "The Sea of Dread breaks about my feet. It is midnight. The pentagram fades from the floor—the nine lamps die—the breath of the One at the casement is upon me——"

Vere stopped.

"A handful of pages have been torn out here," he stated. "The next entry that I can read is in the middle of a stained page, and must be considerably later on."

Phillida made an odd little noise like a whimper, clutching at his sleeve. The third shock for which I had been waiting shuddered through the house, this time distinctly enough for all to feel. A gust of wind went through the wet trees outside like a gasp.

"Ethan, what was that?" she stammered. "Oh, I'm afraid! Cousin Roger——?"

I had no voice to answer her. In my ears was the rush and surge of that sea whose waters had gripped me in the past night. I felt the icy death-tide hiss around me in its first returning wave, rise to my knee's height, then sink away down its unearthly beach. What I had dimly known all day, underlying Vere's sturdy cheerfulness and our plans and efforts, was the truth. Through those intervening hours of daylight I had remained my enemy's prisoner, bound on that shore we both knew well, until It pleased or had power to return and finish with me. No doubt It was governed by laws, as we are.

As before, the cold struck a paralysis across my senses. Vere's reassurance sounded faint and distant.

"The thunder is getting closer," he said. "That was a storm wind, all right! Would you rather go upstairs and lie down, and not hear any more of this stuff tonight?"

"No! Oh, no! I could not bear to be alone," she refused. "Just, just go on, dear. Of course it is the coming storm that makes the room so cold."

He put his left arm around her as she nestled against him. His right hand held the diary flattened on the table under the light.

"The next entry is just one line in the middle of a page where everything else is blotted out," Vere repeated. "It reads: 'The child is a week old today.'"

The wave crashed foaming in tumult up the strand, flowing higher, drenching me in cold sharp as fire. The tide rose faster tonight. The silence that held the others dumb before the significance of that last sentence covered my silence from notice. Desire's face was quite hidden; lamplight and firelight wavered and gleamed across her bent head. I wanted to arise and go to her, to take her hands and tell her to have patience and courage. But when this wave ebbed, my strength drained away with the receding water. Moreover, the darkness curdled and moved beyond the window opposite me. The curtains hung between were no bar to my vision, as the light and presence of my companions were no bar to the Thing that kept rendezvous with me. Since last night, we were nearer to one another.

A breath of chill foulness crept across the pungent odor of the burning apple-log in the fireplace. A whisper spoke to my intelligence.

"Man conquered by me, fall down before me. Beg my forbearance. Beg life of me—and take the gift!"

"No," my thought answered Its.

"You die, Man."

"All men die."

"Not as they die who are mine."

"I am not yours. You kill me, as a wild beast might. But I am not yours; not dying nor dead am I yours."

"Would you not live, pygmy?"

"Not as your pensioner."

The logs on the hearth crackled and sank down with a soft rustle, burned through to a core of glowing red. Phillida spoke with a hushed urgency, drawing still closer to her husband, so that her forehead rested against his shoulder.

"Go on, Ethan. Finish and let us be done."

Vere bent his head above the book on the table to obey her. Across the dark I suddenly saw the Eyes glare in upon him.

"On the next page, the writing begins again," he said. "It says:

"'I am offered the kingdoms of earth. But I crave that kingdom of myself which I cast away. The child is sent to England. The circle is drawn. The names are traced and the lamps filled. Tonight I make the last essay. There remains untried one mighty spell. This Mystery — —'"

A clap of thunder right over the house overwhelmed the reader's voice. Phillida screamed as a violent wind volleyed through the place with a crashing of doors and shutters, upstairs and down. The diary was ripped from beneath Vere's hand and hurled straight to the center of that nest of fire formed by the settling of the logs. A long tongue of flame leaped high in the chimney as the spread leaves of the book caught and flared, fanned by wind and draft. Vere sprang up, but Phillida's clinging arms delayed him. When he reached the fire-tongs there was nothing to rescue except a charring mass half-way toward ashes.

He turned toward me, perhaps at last surprised by my immobility.

"I am sorry, Mr. Locke," he apologized.

Desire had started up with the others when the sudden uproar of the storm burst upon them. Now she cried out, breaking Vere's excuse of the loss. Her small face blanched, she ran a few steps toward me.

"It has come! He will die—he is dying. Look, look!"

CHAPTER XX

"Behold! Where are their abodes?
Their places are not, even as though they had not been."

—TOMB OF KING ENTEF.

Desire Michell was beside me, and I could not rise or answer her. She bent over me, so that the Rose of Jerusalem fragrance inundated me and drove back the sickening air that was the breath of our enemy.

"Let me go," she sobbed, her head beside my head. "If you can hear me, listen and leave me as It wills. You know now that I belong to It by heritage? You know why we can never be together as you planned? Try to feel horror of me. Put me away from you. No evil can come to me unless I seek evil. But It will not suffer you to take me. Live, dear Roger, and let me go."

"Yield to me, Man, what you may not keep," the whisper of the Thing followed after her voice. "Would you take the witch-child to your hearth? Cast her off; and taste my pardon."

"Can you hear, Roger? Roger, let me go."

With an effort terrible to make as death to meet, I broke from the paralysis that chained me. As from the drag of a whirlpool, I tore myself from the tide-clutch, from the will of the Thing, from the numb weakness upon me. For a moment I thrust back the hand at my throat. I stood up and drew Desire up with me in my arms, both of us reeling with my unsteadiness.

"I do not give you up," I said, my speech hoarse and difficult. "I claim you, now, and after. And my claim is good, because I pay."

Desire exclaimed something. What, I do not know. Her voice was lost in the triumphant conviction that I was right. She was free, and the freedom was my gift to her. I was not vanquished, but victor. The life I paid was not a penalty, but a price.

Her face was uplifted to mine as she clung to me; then my weight glided through her arms and I fell back in my chair.

I was alone amid blackness and desolation that poured past me like the wind above the world.

For the last time, I opened my eyes on the gray shore at the foot of the Barrier. I, pygmy indeed, stood again before the colossal wall whose palisades reared up beyond vision and stretched away beyond vision on either side.

I was alone here. No whisper of taunt or menace, no presence of horror troubled me. Opposite me, the Breach that split the cliff showed as a shadowed cañon, empty except of dread. Far out behind me the sea that was like no sea of earth gathered itself beneath its eternal mists as a tidal wave draws and gathers. With folded arms I stood there, waiting for the returning surge of mighty waters to overwhelm me in their flood. I waited in awe and solemn expectancy, beyond fear or hope.

But now I became aware of a new doubleness of experience. Here on the Frontier, I was between the worlds, yet I also saw the room in the house left behind. I saw myself as an unconscious body reclined in a chair beside the hearth. Desire Michell knelt on the floor beside me, her hands grasping my arms, her gaze fixed on my face, her hair spilling its shining lengths across my knees. Phillida was huddled in a chair, crying hysterically. Vere apparently had been trying to force some stimulant upon the man who was myself, yet was not myself, for while I watched he reluctantly rose from bending above the figure and set a glass upon the table. I echoed his sigh. Life was good.

The sea behind me began to rush in from immeasurable distances. The roar of the waters' thunderous approach blended with the heat and flash of storm all about the house into which I looked.

"He dies," Desire spoke, her voice level and calm. "Has it not been so with all who loved the daughters of my race these two centuries past? Yet never did one of those die as he dies—not for passion, but for protection of the woman—not as a madman or one ignorant, but facing that which was not meant for man to face, his eyes beating back the intolerable Eyes. Oh, glory and grief of mine to have seen this!"

Phillida cowered lower in her chair, burying her face in the cushions. But Vere abruptly stood erect, his fine dark face lifted and set. Just so some ancestors of his might have risen in a bleak New England meeting-house when moved powerfully to wrestle with evil in prayer. But it is doubtful if any Maine deacon ever addressed his Deity as Vere appealed to his.

"Almighty, we're in places we don't understand," he spoke simply as to a friend within the room, his earnest, drawling speech entirely natural. "But You know them as You do us. If things have got to go this way, why, we'll make out the best we can. But if they don't, and we're just blundering into trouble, please save Roger Locke and this poor girl. Because we know You can. Amen."

Now at this strange and beautiful prayer—or so it seemed to me—a ray of blinding light cleaved up from where Vere stood, like a shot arrow speeding straight through house and night into inconceivable space. Then the room vanished from my sight as the great wave burst out of the mist upon me.

I went down in a smother of ghastly snarling floods cold as space is cold. Something fled past me up the strand, shrieking inhuman passion; the Eyes of my enemy glared briefly across my vision.

One last view I glimpsed of that dread Barrier, amid the tumult and welter of my passing. The breach was closed! Unbroken, majestic, the enormous Wall stood up inviolate.

CHAPTER XXI

"Fancy, like the finger of a clock,
Runs the great circuit, and is still at home."

—COWPER.

The uproar of rushing waters was still in my ears. But I was in my chair before the hearth in the living room of the farmhouse, and the noise was the din of a tempest outside.

Opposite me, Phillida and Desire were clinging together, watching me with such looks of gladness and anxiety that I felt myself abashed before them. Bagheera, the cat, sat on the table beside the lamp, yellow eyes blinking at each flash and rattle of lightning and thunder, while he sleeked his recently wetted fur. Wondering where that wet had come from, I discovered presently that the fire was out, and the hearth drenched with soot-stained water. I looked toward the windows, from which the curtains had been drawn aside. Rain poured glistening down the panes, but the clean storm was empty of horror.

"Drink some of this, Mr. Locke," urged Vere, whose arm was about me. "Sit quiet, and I guess you'll be all right in a few moments."

I took the advice. Strength was flowing into me, as inexplicably as it had flowed away from me a while past. How can I describe the certainty of life that possessed me? The assurance was established, singularly enough, for all of us. None of my companions asked, and I myself never doubted whether the danger might return. The experience was complete, and closed. Moreover, already the Thing that had been our enemy, the horror that had been Its atmosphere, the mystery that haunted Desire—all were fading into the past. The phantoms were exorcised, and the house purified of fear.

But there was something different from ordinary storm in this tempest. The tumult of rain and wind linked another, deeper roar with theirs. The house quivered with a steady trembling like a bridge over which a train is passing. Pulling myself together I turned to Vere.

"What is happening outdoors?" I asked.

"The cloudburst was too much for the dam," he answered regretfully. "It went off with a noise like a big gun, a while back. I expect the lake is flooding the whole place and messing up everything from our cellar to the chickenhouse. Daylight is due pretty soon, now, and the storm is dying down. We'll be able to add up the damage, after a bit."

"The water came down the chimney and drowned Bagheera," Phillida bravely tried to summon nonchalance. "Isn't it lucky you and Desire could not get started in the car, after all? Fancy being out in that!"

Desire Michell steadied her soft lips and gave her quota to the shelter of commonplace speech we raised between ourselves and emotions too recently felt.

"It was like the tropical storms in Papua, where I lived until this year," she said. "Once, one blew down the mission house."

Vere's weather prediction proved quite right. In an hour the storm had exhausted itself, or passed away to other places. Sunrise came with a veritable glory of crimson and gold, blazing through air washed limpidly pure by the rain. The east held a troop of small clouds red as flamingoes flying against a shining sky; last traces of our tempest.

We stood on the porch together to survey an unfamiliar scene in the rosy light. Water overlay lawns and paths, so the house stood in a wide, shallow lake whose ripples lapped around the white cement steps and the pillars of the porte-cochère. Phillida's Pekin ducks floated and fed on this new waterway as contentedly as upon their accustomed pastures. Small objects sailed on the flood here and there; Bagheera's milk-pan from the rear veranda bobbed amidst a fleet of apples shaken down in the orchard, while some wooden garden tools nudged a silk canoe-cushion.

In contrast to all this aquatic prospect, where the real lake had been there now lay some acres of ugly, oozing marsh; its expanse dotted with the bodies of dead water-creatures and such of Vere's young trout as had not been swept away by the outpouring flood. The dam was a mere pile of débris through which trickled a stream bearing no resemblance to the sparkling waterfall of yesterday. Already the sun's rays were drawing a rank, unwholesome vapor from the long-submerged surface.

We contemplated the ruin for a while, without words.

"Poor Drawls!" Phillida sighed at length. "All your work just rubbed out!"

"Never mind, Vere," I exclaimed impulsively. "We will put it all back in the same shape as it was."

But even as I spoke, I felt an odd shock of uneasiness and recoil from my own proposition. I did not want the lake to be there again; or to hear the unaccountable sounds to which it gave birth and the varying fall of the cataract over the dam. Did the others share my repugnance? I seemed to divine that they did. Even the impetuous Phil did not break out in welcome of my offer. Desire, who had smoothed her sober gray dress in some feminine fashion and stood like Marguerite or Melisande with a great braid over either shoulder, moved as if to speak, then changed her intention. A faint distress troubled her expression.

As usual, Vere himself quietly lifted us out of unrest.

"I'm not sure that couldn't be bettered, Mr. Locke," he demurred. "That is if you liked, of course! That marsh could be cleaned up and drained into pretty rich land, I guess. And down there beyond the barn, on the other side where the creek naturally widens out into a kind of basin, I should think might be the spot for a smaller, cleaner lake."

"Doesn't it seem to you, Ethan," I said, "that we have progressed rather past the *Mr. Locke* stage?"

A little later, when Desire and I were alone on the porch, we walked to the end nearest the vanished lake. Or rather, I led her to a swinging couch there, and sat down beside her.

"Point out the path down the hill by which you used to come," I asked of her.

She shook her head. There are no words to paint how she looked in the clear morning, except that she seemed its sister.

"It is only the end of a path that matters," she said. "Look instead at the marsh. Do you see nothing there stranger than a path through the woods even when trodden by a wilful woman?"

Following her lifted finger, I saw a series of long mounds out there in the muddy floor not far from the dam. Not high, two or three feet at most, the mounds formed an irregular square of considerable area.

"The old house!" I exclaimed.

"It was set on fire by the second Desire Michell one night deep in winter. Her father built this house of yours and put in the dam that covered the ruins with water. I think he hoped to wash away the horror upon the place."

"I know so little of your history."

"You can imagine it." She turned her head from me. "The first child came back from England when it was a man grown, and claimed the house and name of the first Desire. He settled and married here. For two generations only sons were born to the Michells. I do not know if the Dark One came to them. I believe it did, but they were hard, austere men who beat off evil. Then, a daughter was born. She looked like the first Desire and she was—not good. She was a scandal to the family. She listened to It— —! The tradition is that she set fire to the house after a terrible quarrel with her people, but herself perished by some miscalculation. There were no more girls born for another while after that. Not until my father's time. He had a sister who resembled the two Desires of the past. My grandfather brought her up in harshness and austerity, holding always before her the wickedness to which she was born. Yet it was no use. She fled from his house with a man no one knew, and died in Paris after a life of great splendor and heartlessness. Everyone who loved the Desires suffered. That is why I—covered myself from—you."

I took her hand, so small a thing to hold and feel flutter in mine.

"But what of me, Desire? The darkness covered no beauty in me, but a defect. You never saw me until last night and now in the morning. Now that you know, can you bear with a man who—limps? You, so perfect?"

She turned toward me. Her kohl-dark eyes, vivid as a summer noon, opened to my anxious scrutiny.

"But I have seen you often," she said, the heat of confession bright on cheek and lip. "I never meant you to know, but now — —! After the first time you spoke to me so kindly and gayly—I was so very sorrowfully alone—and the convent was so dull! My father's field-glasses were in my trunk."

"Desire?"

"I fear I have no vocation for a nun. I—there is a huge rock half-way down the hill with a clear view of this place. I have spent hours there, watching these lawns and verandas, and the things you all did. It all seemed so amusing and, and happy. You see, where I lived there were almost no white people except my father and a priest at the Catholic mission. So I learned to know Phillida and Mr. Vere and——"

"Then, all this time, Desire——"

"The glasses brought you very close," she whispered. "I knew you by night and by day."

CHAPTER XXII

"Life hath its term, the assembly is dispersed,
And we have not described Thee from the first."

—GULISTAN.

I have come to the end of this narrative and with the end, I come to what people of practical mind may call its explanation. Of the four of us who were joined in living through the events of that summer, my wife and I and Ethan Vere agree in one belief, while Phillida holds the opinion of her father, the Professor. I think Bagheera, the cat, might be added to our side also, if his testimony was available.

The press reports of the cloudburst and flood brought the Professor up to Connecticut to verify with his own eyes his daughter's safety. Aunt Caroline did not come with him, but I may here set down that she did come later. They found their son-in-law by no means what their forebodings menaced, so reconciled themselves at last to the marriage; to Phillida's abiding joy.

But first the little Professor arrived alone, three days after the storm. Characteristically, he had sent no warning of his coming, so no one met him at the railway station. He arrived in one of those curious products of a country livery stable known as a rig, driven by a local reprobate whom no prohibition could sober.

I shall never forget the incredulous rapture with which Phillida welcomed him, nor the pride with which she presented Vere.

The damages to the place were already being repaired, although weeks of work would be needed to restore a condition of order and make the changes we planned. The automobile had been disentangled from the wreckage of garage and willow tree and towed away to receive expert attention. We were awaiting the arrival of the new car I had ordered for the honeymoon tour Desire and I were soon to take. Phillida had declared two weeks shopping a necessary preliminary to the wedding of a bride who was to live in New York "and meet everybody." Nor would I have shortened the pretty orgy into which the two girls entered, transforming my sorceress into a lady of the hour; happiness seeming to me rather to be savored than gulped.

Needless to say, there was no more talk of the convent whose iron gates were to have closed between the last Desire Michell and the world. She had been directed there by the priest whose island mission was near her father's. In her solitude and ignorance of life, the sisterhood seemed to offer a refuge in which to keep her promise to her father. But she had to learn the principles of the Church she was about to adopt, and during that period of delay I had come to the old house.

On the second day of his visit, we told all the story to the Professor. We could not have told Aunt Caroline, but we told him.

"It is perfectly simple," he pronounced at the end. "Interesting, even unique in points, but simple of explanation."

"And what may be the explanation?" I inquired with scepticism.

"Marsh gas," he replied triumphantly. "Have none of you young people ever considered the singular emanations from swamps and marshes where rotting vegetation underlies shallow water? Phillida, I am astonished that you did not enlighten your companions on this point. You, at least, have been carefully educated, not in the light froth of modern music and art, but in the rudiments of science. I do not intend to wound your feelings, Roger!"

"I am not wounded, sir," I retorted. "Just incredulous!"

"Ah?" said the Professor, with the bland superiority of his tribe. "Well, well! Yet even you know something of the evils attending people who live in low, swampy areas; malaria, ague, fevers. In the tropics, these take the form of virulent maladies that sweep a man from earth in a few hours. Your lake *was* haunted, so was the house that once stood in its basin, as some vague instinct strove to warn the generations of Michells as well as you. Haunted by emanations of some powerful form of marsh gas given forth more plentifully at night, which lowered the heart action and impeded the breathing of one drawing the poison into his lungs through hours of sleep, producing—nightmare. Science has by no means analyzed all the possibilities of such phenomena."

"Nightmare!" I cried. "Do you mean to account by nightmare for the wide and repeated experiences that twice brought me to the verge of death? And Desire? What of her knowledge of that same nightmare? What of the legend of her family so exactly coinciding with all I felt? And why did not Phillida and Ethan suffer the nightmare with me?"

He held up a lean hand.

"Gently, gently, Roger! Consider that of all the household you alone slept in the side of the house toward the lake. I know that you always have your windows open day and night—a habit that used to cause great annoyance to your Aunt Caroline when you were a boy. Thus you were exposed to the full effect of the water gases. That you did not feel the effects every night I attribute to differences in the wind, that from some directions would blow the fumes away from the house, thus relieving you. I gather from your account that the phenomena were most pronounced in close, foggy weather, when the poisonous air was atmospherically held down to the earth. You have spoken of miasmic mists that hung below the level of the tree-tops. When Mr. Vere experienced a similar unease and depression, he was on the shore of the lake at dawn after precisely such a close, foggy night as I have described as most dangerous. The symptoms confirm this theory. You say you awakened on each occasion with a sense of suffocation. Your heart labored, your limbs were cold and mind unnaturally depressed, owing to slow circulation of the blood. You were a man asphyxiated. After each attack you were more sensitive to the next, as a malaria patient grows worse if he remains in the swamp districts. It is remarkable that you did not guess the truth from the smell of decaying vegetation and stagnant damp which you admit accompanied the seizures! However, you did not; and in your condition the last three days of continuous fog brought on two attacks that nearly proved fatal. Now as to the character of your hallucinations, and their agreement with the young lady's ideas. That is a trifle more involved discussion, yet simple, simple!"

He put the tips of his fingers together and surveyed us with the benign condescension of one instructing a class of small children.

"The first night that you passed in your newly purchased house, Roger, you accidentally encountered Miss Michell; or she did you!" He smiled humorously. "While your feelings were excited by the unusual episode, the strange surroundings and the dark, she related to you a wild legend of witchcraft and monsters. Later, when you suffered your first attack of marsh-gas poisoning, your consequent hallucination took form from the story you had just heard. Later conversations with your mysterious lady fixed the idea into an obsession. Recurrent dreams are a common phenomenon even in healthy persons. In this case, no doubt the exact repetition of the physical sensations of miasmic poisoning tended to reproduce in your mind the same sequence of ideas or semi-delirious imaginings. These were of course varied or distorted somewhat on each occasion, influenced by what you had been hearing or reading in advance of them. This mental condition became more and more confirmed as you steeped yourself more deeply in legendary lore and also—pardon me—in the morbid fancies of the young lady; whose ghostly visits in the dark and whose increasing interest for you put a further bias upon your thoughts."

"What were the noises I heard from the lake, and the shocks we all felt?" I demanded.

He nodded amiably toward Vere.

"Mr. Vere has mentioned the large bubbles which formed and burst on the surface of the lake. That is a common manifestation of ordinary marsh gas. Possibly the singular and unknown emanation that took place at night came to the surface in the form of a bubble or bubbles huge enough to produce in bursting the smacking sound of which you speak. But I am inclined to another theory, after a walk I took about your place this morning. When you put up your cement dam instead of the old log affair that held back only a part of the stream, you made a greater depth and bulk of water in the swamp basin than it has contained these many years, if ever. As a result, I believe the sloping mud basin began to slip toward the dam. Oh, very gradually! Probably not stirring for weeks at a time. Just a yielding here, a parting there, until the cloudburst precipitated the disaster. You had, my dear Roger, a miniature landslide, which would account for sounds of shifting mud and water in your lake, and for the shocks or trembling of your house when the earth movements occurred."

The rest of us regarded one another. I think Vere might have spoken, if he had not been unwilling to mar Phillida's contentment by any appearance of dispute with her father.

"It is very cleverly worked out, sir," I conceded. "But how do you explain that Desire knew what I experienced with the Thing from the Barrier, if my experiences were merely delirious dreams?"

"I have not yet understood that she did know," said the Professor dryly. "She put the suggestions into your head; innocently, of course. When you afterward compared notes and found they agreed, you cried 'miraculous'! How is that, Miss Michell? Did you actually know what Roger experienced in these excursions before he told you of them?"

Desire gazed at him with her meditative eyes, so darkly lovely, yet never quite to lose their individual difference from any other lovely eyes I have ever seen. The eyes, I thought then and still think, of one who has seen more, or at least seen into farther spaces, than most of treadmill-trotting humanity. She wore one of the new frocks for which Phillida and she had already made a flying trip to town; a most sophisticated frock from Fifth Avenue, with frivolous French shoes to correspond. Her hair of a Lorelei was demurely coiled and wound about her little head. Yet some indescribable atmosphere closed her delicately around, an impalpable wall between her and the commonplace. Even the desiccated, material Professor was aware of this influence and took off his spectacles uneasily, wiped them and put them on again to contemplate her.

"I am not sure," she answered him with careful candor. "I believe that I could always tell when the Dark One had been with him. I could feel that, here," she touched her breast. "I knew what its visits were like, because I was brought up to know by my father and was told the history of the three Desire Michells. My father had studied deeply and taught me—I shall not tell anyone all he taught me! I do not want to think of those things. Some of them I have told to Roger. Some of them are quite harmless and pleasant, like the secret formula for making the Rose of Jerusalem perfume; which has virtues not common, as Roger can say who has felt it revive him from faintness. But there are places into which we should not thrust ourselves. It is like—like suicide. One's mind must be perverted before certain things can be done. And that is the true sin—to debase one's soul. All men discover and learn of science and the universe by honest duty and effort is good, is lofty and leads up. Nothing is forbidden to us. But if we turn aside to the low door which only opens to crime and evil purpose, we step outside. I am unskilful; I do not express myself well."

"Very well, young lady," the Professor condescended. "Unfortunately, your theories are wild mysticism. The veritable fiend that has plagued the house of Michell is the mischievous habit of rearing each generation from childhood to a belief in doom and witchcraft. A child will believe anything it is told. Why not, when all things are still equally wonderful to it? Let me point out that your theory also contradicts itself, since Roger certainly did not enter upon any path of crime, yet he met your unearthly monster."

"Because he chose to link his fate with mine, who am linked by heredity with the Dweller at the Frontier," she said earnestly. "He was in the position of one who enters the lair of a wild beast to bring out a victim who is trapped there. It may cost that rescuer his life. Roger nearly paid his life. But he mastered It and took me away from It, because he was not afraid and not seeking his own good. I never imagined anyone so brave and strong and unselfish as Roger. I suppose it is because he thinks of others instead of himself, which gives the strongest kind of strength."

"The Thing nearly had me, though," I hastily intervened to spare my own modesty. "And It did have me worse than afraid!"

"I seem to be arguing against an impenetrable obstinacy," snapped the Professor. "Do you, Roger, who were educated under my own eye, in my house, have the effrontery to tell me that you believe Miss Michell is descended from the union of an evil spirit and a human being; as the Eastern legends claim for Saladin the Great?"

"Your own theory, sir, being — —?" I evaded.

"There is no theory about the matter," he declared. "Excuse me, Miss Michell! The child was undoubtedly Sir Austin's son. Which accounts for the madness of the first Desire Michell."

We were all silent for a while. Whatever thoughts each held remained unvoiced.

"Come, Phillida, you take my sane point of view, I hope?" the Professor finally challenged his daughter, with a glance of scorn and compassion at the rest of our group. "You observe that I have explained every point raised, Miss Michell's testimony being of the vaguest?"

"Yes, Papa," Phillida agreed hesitatingly. "I do believe you have solved the whole problem. Only, if Cousin Roger was suffering from marsh-gas poisoning last night when he seemed to be dying, I do not quite see why Ethan's prayer should have cured him."

The Professor was momentarily posed. He looked disconcerted, took off his glasses and put them on again, and at length muttered something about storm-wind dissipating the miasma in the air and events being mere coincidence.

The house was never again visited by the Dark Presence. Phantom or fancy, the horror was gone as if it never had brooded about the place. Desire Locke is a fatal companion only to my heart.

But whether all this is so because the lake is drained and the Shetland pony of a young Vere browses over the green pasture that was once a miasmic swamp; or whether it is so for more subtle, wilder reasons, no one can say. I, recalling that colossal Barrier I visioned as closed and a certain cleaving arrow of light, must at least call the coincidence amazing.

As I have said, my wife and I, Ethan Vere and Bagheera the cat have an understanding between us.

Lector House believes that a society develops through a two-fold approach of continuous learning and adaptation, which is derived from the study of classic literary works spread across the historic timeline of literature records. Therefore, we aim at reviving, repairing and redeveloping all those inaccessible or damaged but historically as well as culturally important literature across subjects so that the future generations may have an opportunity to study and learn from past works to embark upon a journey of creating a better future.

This book is a result of an effort made by Lector House towards making a contribution to the preservation and repair of original ancient works which might hold historical significance to the approach of continuous learning across subjects.

HAPPY READING & LEARNING!

LECTOR HOUSE LLP
E-MAIL: lectorpublishing@gmail.com

9 789353 429256

Printed in July 2019
by Rotomail Italia S.p.A., Vignate (MI) - Italy